"You're right, there is a lot you don't know. I explained that I'm not at liberty to give you all the details at this time. I have my—"

"I don't care about your orders." She grabbed him by the shirtfront and tried shaking him, maybe to make him see she wasn't taking no for an answer. All she succeeded in doing was sending him teetering closer to the edge. "Tell me the truth, Lyle."

There was no time to develop an intelligent strategy to outmaneuver this precarious situation. No evasive explanation that would satisfy her. His only alternative was distraction.

His fingers dove into her hair. He pulled her mouth up to his and kissed her, hard at first out of sheer desperation, and then softer…because the taste of her melted him from the inside out. To his surprise, she didn't resist.

DEBRA WEBB

COLBY LAW

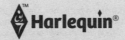

TORONTO NEW YORK LONDON
AMSTERDAM PARIS SYDNEY HAMBURG
STOCKHOLM ATHENS TOKYO MILAN MADRID
PRAGUE WARSAW BUDAPEST AUCKLAND

I want to thank the readers for their love and support of the Colby Agency through all these years!
It's hard to believe that the third book in this trilogy heralds the 50th installment of the Colby Agency!
Enjoy!

Recycling programs for this product may not exist in your area.

ISBN-13: 978-0-373-69614-7

COLBY LAW

Copyright © 2012 by Debra Webb

ABOUT THE AUTHOR

Debra Webb wrote her first story at age nine and her first romance at thirteen. It wasn't until she spent three years working for the military behind the Iron Curtain and within the confining political walls of Berlin, Germany, that she realized her true calling. A five-year stint with NASA on the space shuttle program reinforced her love of the endless possibilities within her grasp as a storyteller. A collision course between suspense and romance was set. Debra has been writing romance suspense and action-packed romance thrillers since. Visit her at www.debrawebb.com or write to her at P.O. Box 4889, Huntsville, AL 35815.

Books by Debra Webb

HARLEQUIN INTRIGUE

934—THE HIDDEN HEIR*
951—A COLBY CHRISTMAS*
983—A SOLDIER'S OATH**
989—HOSTAGE SITUATION**
995—COLBY VS. COLBY**
1023—COLBY REBUILT*
1042—GUARDIAN ANGEL*
1071—IDENTITY UNKNOWN*
1092—MOTIVE: SECRET BABY
1108—SECRETS IN FOUR CORNERS
1145—SMALL-TOWN SECRETS‡
1151—THE BRIDE'S SECRETS‡
1157—HIS SECRET LIFE‡
1173—FIRST NIGHT*
1188—COLBY LOCKDOWN†††
1194—COLBY JUSTICE†††
1216—COLBY CONTROL‡‡
1222—COLBY VELOCITY‡‡
1241—COLBY BRASS‡‡‡
1247—COLBY CORE‡‡‡
1270—MISSING†
1277—DAMAGED†
1283—BROKEN†
1307—CLASSIFIED††
1313—DECODED††
1347—COLBY LAW***

*Colby Agency
**The Equalizers
‡Colby Agency: Elite Reconnaissance Division
†††Colby Agency: Under Siege
‡‡Colby Agency: Merger
‡‡‡Colby Agency: Christmas Miracles
†Colby Agency: The New Equalizers
††Colby Agency: Secrets
***Colby, TX

CAST OF CHARACTERS

Lyle McCaleb—A former security specialist, Lyle jumps at the opportunity to work at the Colby Agency's new Houston office. He never dreamed his first assignment would take him back to his hometown and the girl he'd left behind.

Sadie Gilmore—She has enough trouble on her hands trying to take care of the horses she rescues. When the only man she has ever loved shows up at her door telling her he's there to protect her, she aims her shotgun in true Sadie fashion and orders him off her property.

Gus Gilmore—Sadie is his only daughter but Gus has been keeping a dark secret for a very long time. That secret may prove the death of him and maybe his daughter.

Billy Sizemore—The rodeo star has a secret or two of his own.

Sheriff Cox—He knows which side his bread is buttered on, but will that prevent him from upholding the law?

Janet Tolliver—She holds the key to many dark, dangerous secrets.

Rafe and Clare Barker—The Princess Killers. Which of them is really the cold-blooded murderer? The one on death row or the one recently released?

Tony Weeden—Who is he loyal to? Rafe? Clare? Or himself?

Victoria Colby-Camp—She and Lucas are supposed to be retired, but there is something about this case that just won't let them go.

Lucas Camp—He fears Victoria is being drawn into an emotional war that no one can win.

Simon Ruhl—The head of the new Colby, Texas, agency.

Chapter One

May 20, 9:30 a.m., Polunsky Prison,
Polk County, Texas

Victoria Colby-Camp waited in the cold, sterile room for the man who had requested her presence. Considerable persuasion from the right source had been required to sway the warden of Polunsky Prison to allow this meeting. Lucas, Victoria's husband, though fully retired from his lifelong career with the CIA, still wielded a great deal of influence. One call to the esteemed governor of Texas and Victoria had almost immediate approval to meet with the prison's most infamous death-row inmate.

Raymond Rafe Barker had spent twenty-two years in prison, seventeen on death row, quite an extended period for Texas, where the punishment of heinous criminals was generally carried out in a swift and efficient manner. Many had hoped that the delays would provide the necessary time for him to grow a conscience and give up the locations of the bodies of his victims that were never recovered. But that hadn't happened, and now his time on this earth was coming to a close. In thirty days he would be executed by lethal injection.

Victoria was torn by what she had read in the file provided by the warden and what she might be about to learn. No one wanted to be used as a conduit for an evil man's purposes. Yet, after due consideration of the letter Barker had written, she could not refuse the request.

The door of the interview room opened. Victoria jerked from her troubling thoughts and mentally fortified for the impact of meeting the man whose stunning invitation had brought her here. Two prison guards escorted Barker into the room. The leg irons around his ankles and belly chain coiled about his waist rattled as he was ushered to the chair directly across the table from her. The nylon glides whispered across the tile floor as the chair was drawn back.

"Sit," one of the guards ordered.

Barker glanced at the man on his left, then followed the instruction given. He settled into the molded plastic chair and faced Victoria. His gaze, however, remained lowered, as if his reflection in the steel tabletop had garnered his undivided attention. The second guard secured the leg irons to a hook on the floor and the ones binding Barker's hands to his waist to the underside of the sturdy table that spanned some three feet between the prisoner and his visitor.

"We'll be right outside, ma'am," the first guard said to Victoria, "if you need anything."

"Thank you. We'll be fine."

When the door had closed behind the guards, Barker finally looked up. The move was slow, cautious, as if he too were braced on some level for what was to come. The twenty-three hours per day confined to his cell showed in the pale skin stretched across his gaunt face; a face that narrowed down to slumped shoulders and rail-thin arms covered by colorless prison garb. But the most glaring aspect of his appearance was the faded brown eyes, dull and listless. There was nothing about this man's presence that exhibited the compassion and desperation of the letter he had written to Victoria. Had she made a mistake in coming?

"I didn't think you'd come."

The rustiness of his voice had her resisting the urge to flinch. His voice croaked with disuse and age far beyond his true years. According to the warden, this was the first time he had broken his silence in more than two decades. Reporters, men of God, bestselling authors, all had urged him to tell his story. He had refused. The measure of restraint required to maintain that vigil in spite of so very many reasons not to was nothing short of astonishing.

"Guess you're wishing you hadn't," he offered before Victoria completed her visual inventory of the man labeled as a heinous monster.

"Your letter was quite compelling." Only two pages, but every word had been carefully chosen to convey the worry and outright fear he professed haunted him. Victoria had no choice but to look into the matter. His assertions, though somewhat vague, carried far too much potential for even greater devastation for all concerned in the Princess Killer case. The idea that the man watching her so intently had been arrested and charged with the murders of more than a dozen young girls held her breath hostage as she waited for his next move.

His throat worked as if the words he intended to utter were difficult to summon. "It's true. All of it."

Victoria kept her hands folded in her lap to ensure there was no perception of superiority. She wanted Barker relaxed and open. Even more, she wanted his full attention on her face, not on her unshackled hands. The eyes were the windows to the soul. If she left this room with nothing else gained, she needed to gauge if there was any possibility whatsoever that he was telling the truth about those horrific murders.

The prospect carried monumental ramifications even beyond the added pain to the families of the victims. Her chest tightened at the conceivability of what his long-awaited words might mean. "Why haven't you come forward with this before now?" Having told the truth at or before trial, for instance. Instead, he had refused to talk from the moment he and his wife were arrested.

Clare Barker, on the other hand, had steadfastly stood by her story that she was innocent. As the investigation of the case had progressed, the bodies of eight young girls, ranging in age from twelve to seventeen, had been recovered, but several others remained missing. Clare insisted that she knew nothing about any of the murders. Her husband, a pillar of the small Texas community rocked by the news, had executed all the heinous murders, at least twelve, without her knowledge, and that gruesome number didn't include those of their three young daughters the morning of the arrest. This would not be the first time a community and even a spouse were totally blindsided. Since the evidence had incriminated both Clare and Rafe, there was the remote chance his sudden claims were, in part, the truth.

But why now? There were only two possibilities. First, and most probable, after numerous appeals, his wife had just been released, exonerated legally if not in the eyes of the citizens of Texas, and he wanted revenge. The less likely scenario was that he actually was innocent. Though he had provided no proof in his letter, there was something in his words that Victoria could not ignore. She had explored the depths of evil many times in her nearly three decades of private investigations. Long ago she had learned to trust her instincts. "There was ample opportunity for you to come forward."

"I had my reasons for not speaking out before." He looked away as he said the words, each of which was imbued with distrust and what sounded more like misery than defensiveness.

A deep calming breath was necessary for Victoria to repress any outward reaction. This man, one painted as a monster by the deeds he had refused to deny more than twenty years ago, despite his frail appearance and imminent death now, held the key to closure for so many. Parents who merely wanted to find peace, to provide a proper resting place for their daughters. The warden, Don Prentice, had urged Victoria to tread carefully here. Barker might very well be looking for a last-minute reprieve. No amount of strength possessed by any human fully abated the natural inclination to keep breathing. That cold, hard reality aside, the families of the victims should not have to go through more agony, particularly unnecessary agony. Prentice was right. Too much misery and loss had been wielded by this man and his wife already. Yet, if there was even the most remote chance he was telling the truth… Victoria had to know and to glean whatever good could come of it.

"Mr. Barker, you asked me to come here. You suggested in your letter that it was a life-and-death matter. If you want my help, I need the truth. All of it. Otherwise, I won't waste my time or *yours.*"

Barker stared at her for so long that Victoria wasn't sure whether he would respond or simply cut his losses and call out for a guard to take him away. There was no mistaking the fear that had trickled into his weary eyes. Her pulse accelerated as the realization sank deep into her bones that the terror she saw was undeniably real. But was it for his own life or was it because he believed, perhaps even harbored some sort of proof, that the real killer of all those children had just gone free?

He took a breath that jerked his upper body as if it was the first deep gasp of oxygen he'd been physically able to inhale since sitting down with her. "I didn't hurt anyone, much less a child. I couldn't." Again he looked away.

"Unless you have irrefutable evidence," Victoria began prudently, "the chances of staying your execution are minimal." If that was his intent, as the warden suggested, Victoria refused to be a pawn in Barker's game. She would not allow the media to use her or the Colby Agency to that end.

"I'm ready to go." He squared his thin shoulders. "Don't waste any time on me. This is not about my guilt or innocence. It's about my children." His lips trembled. "And the others." The craggy features of his face tightened as he visibly fought for composure. "I can't do anything to bring those girls back, and I don't know that the truth would ease nobody's pain. Dead is dead." He moved his head side to side with the defeat that showed in the deep lines forged around his mouth. "But I can't let *her* hurt anyone else, especially my girls."

Despite the anticipation whirling like a biting snow-storm inside her, Victoria kept her expression schooled. "In your letter you claimed your wife was responsible for the murders. All of them." The bodies of their three small daughters had never been found, but neither had those of at least four other victims. As much as Victoria wanted to ask specific questions, she could not risk putting words in his mouth. Over and over in his letter he had insisted his daughters were in danger. Yet not a single shred of evidence supported the theory that the children had survived that final downward spiral the morning of the arrest. In all this time no one had come forward and suggested otherwise. The little girls had vanished, and concrete evidence that a violent act had preceded their disappearance had been documented at trial. What he alluded to in his letter and now, face-to-face, had to be supported by something tangible. He needed to say the words without a visible or audible prompt by Victoria.

"That's the truth," Barker repeated, the defeat she'd seen and heard moments ago now gone. "I can't prove it, don't even want to. But it's so just the same." He blinked, clearing the definable emotion from his eyes. "I didn't beg you to come here to save me. I died in here—" he glanced around the room "—a long time ago. I need you to help my girls."

Now they were getting somewhere. His leading the way was essential. "What exactly is it you're asking me to do?" Did he want her to recover their bodies and ensure a proper burial? If they weren't dead, why would he not want to prove his innocence of those particular charges? Why had he allowed all involved in the case to believe they were deceased? Was he simply trying to muddy the waters? Whatever his end game, Victoria needed him to spell it out. The warden was monitoring this interview, as well he should.

"As far as the world is concerned," Barker explained in that unpracticed voice, "I can stay the devil they believe I am. That doesn't matter to me." His gaze leveled on Victoria with a kind of desperation that sent a chill all the way to her core. "Once I found out *she* was going to get away with what she'd done, it took some time to find just the right person I could trust with what I knew had to be done. Careful research by certain folks in here who knew I needed help."

That this man had developed a loyal following of some sort during his tenure was no surprise, since the warden had not known the contents of Barker's letter until Victoria had shown it to him. The letter had gotten through the prison mail system without the usual inspections.

"But over and over the results they found were the same," Barker continued. "There was only one place that consistently fought for justice and helped those in need without ever falling down on the job or resorting to underhanded deeds in order to accomplish the goal. A place that has never once bragged about its record or used the media for self-serving purposes. That place is the Colby Agency."

Time stopped for one second, then two and three. Victoria didn't dare breathe until he finished.

"I can't pay you a dime, and I know my appreciation means nothing to you." He shrugged. "I'm worse than nothing in the eyes of the world. But if you can ignore what you think of me and just do this one thing, I'll know your agency is everything I read it was." Another of those deep, halting breaths rattled his torso. "I beg you, just protect my girls from *her*. That's all I want."

Victoria's heart thudded hard against her chest, then seemed to still with the thickening air in the room. "I'm sorry, Mr. Barker. You're going to have to be more precise as to what your request involves since *you* pled guilty to murdering your daughters twenty-two years ago. Neither your letter nor what you're saying to me now makes sense."

"They're alive." The words reverberated against the cold, white walls. "My girls are alive."

Adrenaline burned through Victoria's veins. Still she resisted any display of her anticipation. "The first officers on the scene the morning you and your wife were arrested," she countered cautiously, "found blood in the girls' bed. Blood in the trunk of your car along with a teddy bear that your middle daughter carried with her everywhere. The blood was tested and determined to be that of your daughters." Victoria hesitated until the horror of her words stopped darkening his features and echoing in her own ears. "You never denied killing your young children, Mr. Barker. To date there is no evidence to the contrary. In light of those facts, how can you expect me to believe you're finally telling the truth now?"

Fury, undeniable and stark, blazed in his eyes before he quickly smothered it and visibly grabbed back control. "That was to prevent *her* from ever knowing the girls were alive and hurting them somehow to get back at me for setting in motion her discovery." Several moments passed as he discernibly composed himself. "They deserved a chance at a decent life untainted by her poison. I had to make sure that happened."

When Victoria would have responded, he said more. "My daughters are alive and well, and if you don't help me, she will find them and kill them. For real this time." He leaned forward, as close as his shackles would allow, and stared deep into Victoria's eyes. "She's pure evil, and you're the only one I can trust to stop her."

Chapter Two

"He's lying." Warden Don Prentice made his announcement and pushed out of his chair, indicating his already thin patience had reached an end. "You know what this is, and I'm not taking the bait."

Lyle McCaleb waited for a reaction from his boss, Simon Ruhl, head of the Colby Agency's new Houston office, or from the agency's matriarch, Victoria Colby-Camp. Simon exchanged a look with Victoria then turned to the warden. "Mr. Prentice, we genuinely appreciate your indulgence in this matter. I must admit that I concur with your assessment in light of the facts as we know them."

"That said," Victoria continued as if the rebuttal were a well-rehearsed strategy and she was about to play bad cop, "as warden of this institution, you have an obligation to report this theoretical threat to the proper authorities. Our agency does not have that same legal obligation. However, we have a moral one. We cannot just walk away and pretend this incident never happened."

Prentice shoved back the sides of his jacket, planted

his hands on his hips and gave his head a frustrated shake. "Do you have any idea what stirring up this mess in the media will do to those families?" He paced back and forth behind his desk like an inmate in his compact cell. "There's no way to keep it out of the press." Prentice stopped and stared at Victoria, then Simon. "The folks who thrive on this kind of heartache have been waiting for this moment for twenty-two years!"

"I do understand," Simon agreed once more. "That's exactly why I hope you'll see the logic in our proposition."

Lyle figured things could go either way from here. Prentice had agreed to this conference after Victoria's brief meeting with Barker this morning. Three hours had elapsed since that time with Victoria, her husband, Lucas, and Simon organizing a feasible strategy and the necessary resources. Lyle had jumped at the assignment. As the former head of one of Houston's most prestigious security firms, he knew the business of protection, and his tracking skills were top-notch from his days as a county sheriff's deputy. Add to that the fact that he was a lifelong resident of Texas and the combined bonus of high-level connections with a number of those in law enforcement, and he was the best man for the job. Initially, Simon and Victoria had hesitated. Texas was home and perhaps that made him less than objective. Though he'd only been seven at the time of the Barkers' arrest, his parents had followed news of the high-profile case for years after that.

He might not be the most objective investigator on staff, but in his opinion, that deep-seated understanding of how the entire travesty had affected the community as well as the state could prove useful in solving this puzzle. Fortunately, Simon and Victoria had concluded the same.

Lucas was not happy about his wife's insistence on being so deeply involved in this case. Recently retired from the day-to-day operations of the Colby Agency, the two were in Houston for only a few months. Just long enough to get the new office staffed and running efficiently. Simon was clearly more than capable of getting the job done on his own, but Lyle sensed Victoria and Lucas were dragging their feet with the whole retirement thing. Suited him just fine. Lyle was grateful for the opportunity to work with the esteemed Victoria Colby-Camp. Lucas was more or less an unknown to him, but Lyle was acquainted with the Colby name. The moment he'd heard the agency was opening an office in Houston, he was ready to sign on. This would be his first case, and he was itching to get in the field and start proving his value to the agency.

"You have my personal assurance, Mr. Prentice," Victoria said, drawing Lyle's attention back to her and the challenge she would absolutely win, "that this matter will be handled in the most discreet manner. No one outside this room and a select few at my agency will know the details of this case. The Colby Agency's reputation speaks for itself."

Lyle studied the warden's face, analyzed the way the muscles relaxed as he slowly but surely admitted defeat. He wasn't totally convinced, but he had likely done his homework. A guarantee like that from the head of the Colby Agency was the best offer he was going to get. And, as Victoria said, there was no turning back at this point. The cards had been dealt, the wager on the table. Someone had to make the next move.

"If this gets out—"

"It won't," Simon assured the warden. "Not from the Colby Agency."

"How can you protect these children—" Prentice closed his eyes, shook his head in resignation before opening his eyes once more "—these women when you don't know if they're even alive, much less where they are. My God, this is ludicrous."

Lyle wanted to give the man a good, swift kick in the seat of the pants. They were wasting time with all this beating around the bush.

"We already have someone in place monitoring Clare Barker's movements," Simon enlightened Warden Prentice. "We took that measure immediately."

Surprise and confusion cluttered the warden's face. "How is that possible? They took her out of Mountain View in the middle of the night. Half a dozen decoy vehicles were used to elude the media and the horde picketing her release. No one—not even me—knows where she is!"

Lyle had learned quickly that at the Colby Agency the enigmatic Lucas Camp was an ace in the hole. Former CIA, the man had some serious connections of his own. Clare Barker had requested residence in Copperas Cove, north of her former hometown, Austin. Part of Lyle wanted to be the one keeping an eye of the woman, since the Cove was his hometown. But tracking down the truth was his primary goal.

"Be that as it may, Mr. Prentice," Victoria confirmed, "if we could find her so quickly, others will too in time. If this is a game Barker is playing, perhaps his wife is a target and doesn't even realize it. For all we know, she may be the one in danger. Obviously he has some who support his cause. We can provide protection for her in addition to surveillance if the need arises."

"Mr. McCaleb will be tracking down the daughters through the woman Barker claims helped him get the children into hiding." Simon looked from the warden to Lyle and back. "We hope to locate her before the end of the day. Depending on the situation, if the three are indeed alive, we'll assign a bodyguard to keep an eye on each one until this mystery is solved one way or the other."

Prentice held up his hands. "You've made several valid points." He looked directly at Victoria. "Still, the only way I'm agreeing to this is if you keep me posted on your every step." He scrubbed a hand over his face. "That said, I have no choice but to inform the district attorney. If he has a problem with our decision, he and I will work it out." He exhaled a burdened breath. "There's no denying Barker has something up his sleeve, and I don't want any time wasted on bureaucracy. We'll do what we have to do."

Handshakes and more assurances were exchanged before Victoria led the way from Warden Prentice's office. Conversation was out of the question until they exited the facility. As soon as they were back at the agency's offices, Lyle would prepare to move forward. He was champing at the bit, anxious to get down to business putting together the pieces of this bizarre puzzle of depravity.

"When we have Tolliver's address," Victoria said to Lyle, "I want you to approach her as if she represents a flight risk. Slow and easy. If Barker is telling the truth, she has kept this secret for a very long time. She may not be prepared to let go now. Particularly to a stranger."

For the first time since Lyle had met Victoria Colby-Camp he noted uncertainty in those wise, dark eyes. He smiled. "You have my word. But, I have a feeling you believe I have the skills to handle the situation or I wouldn't be here."

Victoria returned the smile. "I just needed to confirm that *you* are as convinced as we are. This case will be anything but simple, I fear."

Lyle imagined he'd have to wake up pretty early in the morning to get a step ahead of this lady.

In the visitors' parking area, Simon hesitated before settling into his sedan. He pulled his cell phone from the interior pocket of his suit jacket and checked the screen before accepting the call. "Ruhl."

Simon Ruhl had the look and the bearing of a lead agent in a Secret Service team rather than a mere P.I., but then this was the Colby Agency. Made sense that Ruhl set the classic high-end example, since he was former FBI. Lyle had never met a federal agent that he cared for until now. Maybe he'd misjudged the whole barrel based on a couple of bad apples. Whatever the case, Simon knew his stuff and Lyle respected him. So far his experience at the Colby Agency was a good fit. The Houston office was nearly fully staffed, and Lyle was impressed with the lineup.

"We're on our way," Simon assured the caller before putting away his cell. "That was Lucas," he said, shifting his attention to Victoria. To Lyle he added, "Janet Tolliver is dead."

Frustration drilled deep into Lyle's gut. "When?" Not five minutes before the meeting with the warden Lucas had notified Simon that Tolliver's last known address was in the process of being confirmed. Prentice had been kept in the dark about this update until the address and the woman's connection to Barker could be verified. This news was seriously going to set back Lyle's efforts to determine if the Barker girls were alive. Janet Tolliver was the only name Barker had given Victoria. Allegedly, she was his co-conspirator in getting the children to safety before the law descended upon the Barkers' modest home in Granger. Tolliver had moved from Austin immediately after that. She'd jumped around for years. Obviously her final location had been found…along with her body.

"Sometime this morning." Simon hit the remote, unlocking his sedan. "A neighbor found her. The police aren't talking yet." Lyle opened the front passenger door for Victoria as Simon continued, "Turns out she had relatives in Copperas Cove. She had moved there just a few months ago. Coincidentally, only a few miles from Clare Barker's new Five Hills address." Simon held Lyle's gaze a moment before tacking on, "your hometown, McCaleb. That may prove the only good thing about this news, as long as you don't have any conflicts with going back home for at least the first step of your investigation."

Lyle shook his head. "No conflicts." None to speak of anyway. He hadn't been *home* in a while. Looked as if that was about to change. He closed Victoria's door and gave Simon a nod. "As soon as we're back at the office I can move out."

No big deal. Lyle had dug up the deads' secrets

before. He could do it again. As long as no one else
died before he got what he needed, he could work with
that.

And, for the record, he didn't believe in coinci-
dences.

11:00 p.m., Copperas Cove

LYLE WAITED IN THE darkness. The local detectives had
finished their initial investigation of the scene and
called it a night. According to his contact, a retired
sheriff's detective, the fifty-eight-year-old woman had
been bludgeoned to death. In spite of that fact, there
was no sign of forced entry, no indication of a true
struggle. A broken lamp, an overturned table, both
the result of her fall, but nothing else, discounting the
blood-stained rug. If not for the blood and the obvious
blows her body had absorbed, she might have merely
suffered a heart attack and crumpled to the floor.

The violent attack came suddenly, unexpectedly,
from a perpetrator Janet Tolliver had known and allowed into her home. The estimated time of death
was between 2:00 and 4:00 a.m. Lucas's contact had
located Clare Barker's position at ten that morning,
moments after Victoria's meeting with Rafe Barker.
Sufficient time for her to have committed the crime,
except that there was no indication she'd left the apartment rented by her attorney not half an hour's drive
from the Tolliver home. Barker had no vehicle as of yet,
and no taxis serving the area had a record of a pickup
at that address during that critical window of time.

Robbery didn't appear to be the motive, since
Tolliver's purse still contained fifty dollars in cash and

her one credit card and none of the usual targets in the home appeared to have been disturbed. Tolliver's great-niece would arrive tomorrow to confirm that presumption and to handle the deceased's final arrangements. The police had not questioned Clare Barker, since they were unaware of any connection between her and Tolliver. Clare's whereabouts between her arrival at her new home at 2:00 a.m. and when Lucas ferreted out her location could not be confirmed beyond the apparent lack of transportation. Seemed pretty damning that Tolliver was dead only a few hours after Barker's release. Even more so since Clare had requested Copperas Cove as her landing point. Had she known about Tolliver? Did this brutal murder confirm Rafe Barker's allegations?

Then again, based on what Lyle had read about Clare in the trial transcripts, she was one sharp cookie. Definitely not the type to act rashly. She'd had a long time to lay out a strategy for life after her release and any revenge she hoped to wield. Seemed to him that she would have taken a bit more care. Then again, anyone involved with murdering young girls couldn't be called logical or rational, and *care* wasn't likely a part of the person's psychological makeup.

Lyle emerged from his truck and locked the doors manually to avoid the *click*. He surveyed the quiet neighborhood until he was satisfied the residents were tucked in for the night. Moonlight and streetlamps washed the eight houses lining this end of the street with a grayish glow. There was only one way in or out, since the street dead-ended here, abutting a copse of trees that flanked the rear parking lot and playground of a school. He hoped his investigation wasn't headed

for a dead end, as well. All the homes were owner occupied. The police had questioned the neighbors. No
one had seen or heard anything. Most of the residents
were older folks. Chances were every last one had been
sound asleep between two and four this morning. By
tomorrow the detectives on the case should be able to
determine if Tolliver had received any phone calls that
might have preceded the late-night visitor.

Since Tolliver was the only person who could
have confirmed Rafe Barker's story, her murder had
changed Lyle's strategy completely. There were a
number of alternative steps he could take. Search the
house, and that was called breaking and entering. Not
to mention tampering with a crime scene. He could
check out any items she might have stored in bank
security-deposit boxes or with an attorney in hopes
a journal or notes of some sort related to her dealings
with Rafe Barker existed. If Lyle played his cards right
he might get an interview with the great-niece, who
could facilitate the other steps on his agenda. A list of
Tolliver's friends, the church she attended and any enemies she might have had would be useful. The down-
side to collecting that kind of information was the time
required, and time was the enemy, on several levels.

He strolled along the sidewalk, studying the modest
architecture with the aid of the streetlamps. Felt strange
to be this close to home without having seen his family
already. The ranch where he'd grown up wasn't far
from Copperas Cove proper. His folks would be disappointed if he didn't stop by and at least say hello. But
stopping by the old home place meant risking running
into *her*. And that was a risk he had no intention of

taking. The longer he was in the Cove, the more that risk increased.

This was not the time to get distracted with ancient history.

Lyle slipped into the darkness at the corner of the last house on the right and moved across the well-manicured back lawns until he reached the home belonging to the victim. Both the front and rear entrances were secured with official crime-scene warnings. A cat crouched on the rear stoop yowled for entrance. Lyle supposed the great-niece would see after any pets now orphaned. Or maybe one of the neighbors would step up to the plate. He'd been lucky so far that no dogs had spotted him or sensed a stranger's presence.

The houses were only a few feet apart, boundaries marked with neatly clipped shrubs. Moving silently, Lyle eased toward the front of the Tolliver house once more, scanning the dark windows as he passed and mentally measuring the distance between the crime scene and the neighbor on this side. Most of the houses were one-story bungalow-style homes. Few had garages or fences, just decades-old shrubs setting the perimeters agreed upon nearly a century ago. Other than the different makes and models of the vehicles in the driveways, one house looked much like the other.

The distinct thwack of a shotgun being racked stopped Lyle dead in his tracks. The threat came from behind him, beyond the row of shrubs.

"I've already called the police."

The voice was female. Older. Steady. No fear. Gave new meaning to the concept of neighborhood watch.

"I don't want any trouble, ma'am." He raised his hands. "I'm going to turn around now."

"You do anything I don't like and I'm shooting," she warned.

Lyle didn't doubt it for a second. "I can guarantee I won't do that, ma'am," he offered. "I grew up in the Cove. Worked as a sheriff's deputy for two years right out of high school."

The elderly woman's gray hair hung over her shoulders. A patchwork robe swaddled her slight body. The shotgun was as big as she was. The streetlamp five or so yards away provided sufficient light for him to see that the lady meant business. Folks in Texas didn't play with guns. If they owned one, they were well versed in how to use it.

"My neighbor was murdered this morning." Her gaze narrowed as she blatantly sized him up. "You got no business prowling around out here in the dark unless you're an officer of the law." She looked him up and down, concluding what she would about his well-worn jeans and tee sporting the Texas Longhorns logo. "You don't look like no cop to me."

"You a friend of Ms. Tolliver's?" He decided not to refer to the victim in the past tense.

"Maybe. What's it to you?"

Well, there was a question he hadn't anticipated.

"I came all the way from Houston to talk to her." He jerked his head toward the crime scene. "I wasn't expecting this. You mind telling me what happened?"

She kept a perfect bead on the center of his chest. "You got a name?"

"Lyle McCaleb."

She considered his name a moment, then shook her head. "I know all Janet's friends, and I've met her niece and her husband. And you ain't none of the above." The lady adjusted her steady hold on the small-gauge shot-gun. "Now, what're you really doing here, and who sent you?"

There was nothing to be gained by hedging the question. She'd called the police. No point avoiding the inevitable. For now there was no confirmed connection between the Barkers and Tolliver, no reason to provide a cover to protect his agenda for now. "I was sent by the Colby Agency, a private investigations firm in Houston."

Something like recognition kicked aside the suspicion in the neighbor's expression and in her posture. She relaxed just a fraction. "Let's see some ID."

Her reaction was something else he hadn't anticipated. There had been a lot of that on this case, and he'd barely scratched the surface of step one. He reached for his wallet.

"My finger's on the trigger, Mr. McCaleb," she warned, "don't make me shoot you."

"Yes, ma'am." He removed his wallet from his back pocket and held it up for her inspection, then opened it and displayed his Colby Agency identification.

She studied the picture ID a moment then lowered the weapon. "Well, all right then. Come on in. I've been waiting for you."

Lyle mentally wrestled back the astonishment that wanted to make an appearance on his face and gave the lady a nod. "Yes, ma'am. After you."

It looked as if surprises were the theme for the night. He parted the shrubs and followed the lady to her front steps and across the porch. At the front door he hesitated. This was beyond strange. She had been waiting for him?

"Come on," she urged, obviously waiting to close the door behind him.

Lyle played along. Why not? A lit lamp on an end table and the discarded newspaper on the sofa suggested she had been up watching television or watching for someone. Seemed a reasonable conclusion that she would be, since after seeing his ID she announced she had been expecting him. Though he couldn't fathom how that was possible.

"Have a seat, Mr. McCaleb." She gestured to the well-used sofa. "I have something for you." And just like that, she disappeared into the darkness around the corner from the dining room.

Not about to put the lady off by ignoring her hospitality, Lyle settled on the sofa. A couple of retirement magazines lay on the coffee table. He picked up one and read the address label. Rhoda Strong. Since this was her address, he assumed his hostess and the subscription recipient were one and the same. Her demeanor certainly matched the surname. To say it was a little out of the ordinary to invite a complete stranger into one's home in the middle of the night after the murder of a neighbor would be a monumental understatement. But then, Ms. Rhoda Strong appeared fully capable of protecting herself.

Still toting her shotgun, the lady of the house returned with an armload of what looked like photo albums.

"You have me at a disadvantage." Lyle stood as she approached the sofa. "I don't know your name."

"Rhoda." She plopped down on the sofa, leaned the shotgun against her right knee and settled the albums in her lap. "Rhoda Strong. Now, sit back down."

"Yes, ma'am." Lyle couldn't wait. Whatever the lady was about to reveal, he didn't want to miss a word. The possibility that she was a brick or two shy of a load poked into the lump of perplexing conclusions taking shape in his head.

"Okay." She huffed as if the whole effort of reaching this point had proved taxing then rested her attention on him. "Don't bother asking me any questions because I have no answers. All I can tell you is that I've known Janet her whole life. She came here from Austin every summer as a kid to spend time at her aunt's house. Janet never married or had any children of her own. She never got into any trouble I know about, but—" she stared down at the albums "—a week ago she said she needed me to keep these three picture books safe for her. She didn't offer any explanations and I didn't ask any questions. I promised her I would and that was that." Her expression turned troubled and distant. "Until yesterday. She come over here and asked if I'd be home all day. Said she might be coming over to get the albums if the company she was expecting arrived. I told her I reckoned I'd be here. Before she left she got this funny look on her face and made me promise one more thing."

Lyle searched the elderly woman's eyes, saw the understanding there that the items she now held had cost her friend her life.

"She made me swear that if anything happened to her I wouldn't go to the police with these pictures or even to her niece. I was to stay right here and be on the lookout for someone. When that someone arrived I was to give these books to that person and that person only."

Before Lyle could assimilate a reasonable response, Rhoda thrust the stack of photo albums at him. He accepted the load that carried far more weight than could be measured in mere pounds and ounces.

"There. I've done what she asked."

Lyle shook his head. "Ms. Strong, I'm confused. There is no way your friend could have known my name."

The older woman shrugged. "Don't suppose she did. She just said someone from the Colby Agency would be coming." She stared straight into his eyes with a certainty that twisted through his chest. "And here you are."

Not ashamed to admit he was rattled, Lyle opened the first of the three albums. Page one displayed a birth certificate for Elizabeth Barker. Parents: Raymond and Clare Barker. His heart pounding, he turned to the next page. A new birth certificate, this one for an Olivia Westfield. There were newspaper clippings and photos, obviously taken without the subject's knowledge, from around kindergarten age to the present. The woman, Olivia, according to her birth certificate was twenty-seven—the oldest of the three missing Barker girls. The second album was the same, Lisa Barker aka Laney Seagers, age twenty-six.

"These are…" Incredible, shocking. No word that came to mind adequately conveyed what he wanted to say. He had to call Simon and Victoria. They had held out some hope of finding Rafe Barker's daughters alive, but this was…mind-blowing.

"I know who they are, Mr. McCaleb," Rhoda said to him, dragging his attention from the carefully detailed history of the Barker children—women. "My friend is dead because she kept this secret all these years. You do whatever you have to do to make sure she didn't die for nothing, and I'll do the same."

"You have my word, ma'am." Adrenaline searing through his blood vessels, Lyle shuffled to the final album. Selma Barker aka Sadie Gilmore.

His heart stopped. *No.* Not possible.

"Yes," Rhoda countered.

Lyle hadn't realized he'd uttered the word aloud until the woman still sitting next to him spoke.

"That one lives right here in Copperas Cove." She tapped the photo of the young woman touted in the newspaper clipping as an animal rights activist. "Do you know her?"

Lyle stared at the face he hadn't seen in seven years, except in his dreams, his gut twisting into knot after knot. "Yes, ma'am. I know her." If he lived a hundred lifetimes, he couldn't forget *this* woman.

Chapter Three

May 21, Second Chance Ranch, 6:30 a.m.

"Get off my ranch." Sadie Gilmore held her ground, feet spread wide apart, the business end of her shotgun leveled on that no-good Billy Sizemore's black heart. Maybe he thought just because he played straw boss for her equally no-good daddy that he could tell her what to do. Not in this lifetime.

Sizemore laughed. Threw his head back so far if he hadn't been holding his designer cowboy hat it would have hit the dirt for sure, and he hooted. This wasn't the first time Sadie had been blazing mad at her daddy's henchmen, especially this knucklehead. Well, she'd had enough. She poked him in the chest with the muzzle of her twenty-gauge best friend. The echo of his laughter died an instant death. A razor-sharp gaze sliced clean through her. She gritted her teeth to conquer a flinch. "Three seconds," she warned, "or I swear I'll risk prison just to see the look on your sorry face when this ball of lead blasts a great big hole in your chest."

"You stole that horse," he accused. "Don't even try denying it."

Sadie was the one who laughed this time. "Prove it."

The standoff lasted another couple of seconds before he surrendered a step. "You'll regret this," he warned, then turned his back to her. It took every speck of self-control she possessed not to shoot him before he reached his dually. But then that would make her the same kind of cheating sneak Gus Gilmore was.

Sadie lowered the barrel of the shotgun she'd inherited from her Grandma Gilmore and let go the breath that had been trapped in her lungs for the past half a minute or so. Sizemore spun away, the tires of his truck sending gravel and dirt spewing through the air and the horse trailer hitched to it bouncing precariously.

"Lying bastard." Billy Sizemore might be a champion when it came to bronc riding, but as a human he scarcely hung on the first link of the food chain, in her opinion. Cow flies had more compassion. Could damn sure be trusted more.

Sadie swiped the perspiration from her brow with the sleeve of her cotton blouse and worked at slowing her heart rate. Usually she didn't let guys like Sizemore get to her, but this time was different. This time the stakes were extra high. No way was she allowing her father to get his way. She'd bought old Dare Devil fair and square. The gelding was done with his rodeo career. Too old to perform for the bronc riders and too riddled with arthritis for chuck wagon races or anything else. Just because Gus claimed the former competition star had been shipped off to the auction by mistake was no concern of hers. Sadie knew exactly what happened to those horses in far too many cases, and she couldn't bear it. Gus didn't need to know that she still had a friend or two on his side of the five-foot barbed wire fence that divided their properties.

"What you don't know won't hurt you, old man," she proclaimed with a hard look to the west before visually tracking Sizemore's big old truck and trailer roaring down the last leg of her half-mile-long drive.

When the dust had settled and the dually was long gone, Sadie walked back to the house. Three furry heads peeked out from under the front porch, big soulful eyes peering up at her hopefully.

"Worthless." She shook her head at the mutts. "That's what you three are."

Gator, the Lab, Frisco, an Australian shepherd mix, and Abigail, a Chihuahua, scurried from their hiding place and padded into the house behind her. That first cup of coffee was long gone, and the lingering scent of the seasoned scrambled eggs she'd turned off fifteen minutes ago had her stomach rumbling. The enemy's arrival had interrupted her peaceful morning.

With her shotgun propped in the corner near the kitchen table, she adjusted the flame beneath the skillet to warm up the eggs. Another more pungent odor sifted through her preoccupation with the sharp gnawing pains in her belly. Smelled like something scorched…

"My biscuits!" Sadie grabbed a mitt and yanked the oven door open. "Well, hell." Not exactly burned but definitely well done and probably as hard as rocks. She plopped the hot tray on the stove top and tossed the mitt aside. How could a grown woman screw up a can of ready-to-bake biscuits? "One who's spent her whole life in the barn," she muttered.

Her mother had passed away before Sadie was old enough to sit still long enough to learn any culinary skills. The rodeo was all her father had bothered to teach her, and most of the lessons she'd gleaned were ones she wanted to forget. Gus Gilmore was heartless. But then, she'd understood that by the time she was fifteen. He'd tried to keep her away from her grandparents when she was a kid, but she always found a way to sneak in a visit. He had worked overtime to keep her away from everything she loved until she was twenty-one. That date had been more than a significant birthday; it had been her personal independence day. Prevented from taking anything from her childhood home other than the clothes on her back, she'd walked into the lawyer's office and claimed the inheritance her grandparents had left for her—despite Gus's every attempt to overturn their will—and hadn't looked back.

Nineteen months later she had created the life she wanted, just outside her father's reach yet right under his nose. They had been at all-out war since. Fact was, they had been immersed in battle most of her life. The stakes had merely been upped with her inheritance. Gus, being an only child, had assumed he would inherit the small five-hundred-acre ranch that adjoined his massive property. But life had a way of taking a man down a notch or two when he got too big for his breeches.

Sadie poured a second cup of morning-survival liquid and savored the one thing in the kitchen she was pretty good at—rich, strong coffee. She divided up the eggs and biscuits with her worthless guard dogs and collapsed at the table. Mercy, she was running behind this morning. If that low-down Sizemore hadn't shown up, she would be feeding the horses already instead of stuffing her face.

First things first. She had to calm down. The animals sensed when she was anxious. And fueling her body was necessary. Gus's pals had intimidated the last of her ranch hands until they'd all quit, leaving Sadie on her own to take care of the place. She didn't mind doing the work, but there was only so much one woman could do between daylight and dark. She'd narrowed her focus to the animals and the necessary property areas, such as the barn and smaller pasture. Everything else that required attention would just have to wait. Things would turn around eventually. As long as she was careful, her finances would hold out. Between the small trust her grandparents had left and donations for taking care of her rescues from generous folks, she would be okay in spite of her daddy's determined efforts to ensure otherwise.

Gator and Frisco stared up at her from their empty bowls. Abigail stared, too, but she hadn't touched her biscuit. Not that Sadie could blame her. Maybe her ranch hands had fled for parts unknown to escape her cooking. Sadie didn't like to waste anything, unlike Gus, so the dogs were stuck with her cooking until she figured out how to prepare smaller portions.

Before she could shovel in the final bite of breakfast, all three dogs suddenly stilled, ears perked, then the whole pack made a dash for the front door. Sadie pushed back her chair, her head shaking in disgust. If Gus had decided to show up in person and add his two cents' worth, he might just leave with more than he bargained for. Or maybe less, depending upon how well her trigger-finger self-control held out.

Shotgun in hand, she marched to the door and peeked out around the curtains her grandmother had made when Sadie was a little girl. The black truck wasn't one she recognized. Too shiny and new to belong to any of the ranchers around here, at least the ones who actually worked for a living. Ten or so seconds passed and the driver didn't get out. The way the sun hit the windshield, it was impossible to tell if the driver was male or female, friend or foe.

She opened the door and the dogs raced toward the truck, barking and yapping as if they were a force to be reckoned with. If the driver said a harsh word, the three would be under the porch in a heartbeat. Sadie couldn't really hold it against them. All three were rescues. After what they'd gone through, they had a right to be people shy.

With the shotgun hanging at her side, she made it as far as the porch steps when the driver's door opened. Sadie knew the deputies in Coryell County. Her visitor wasn't any of them. A boot hit the ground, stirring the dust. Something deep inside her braced for a new kind of trouble. As the driver emerged her gaze moved upward, over the gleaming black door and the tinted window to a black Stetson and dark sunglasses. She couldn't quite make out the details of the man's face, but some extra sense that had nothing to do with what she could see set her on edge.

Another boot hit the ground and the door closed. Her visual inspection swept over long legs cinched in comfortably worn denim, a lean waist and broad shoulders testing the seams of a shirt that hadn't come off the rack at any store where she shopped, finally zeroing in on the man's face just as he removed the dark glasses.

The weapon almost slipped from her grasp. Her heart bucked hard twice then skidded to a near halt.

Lyle McCaleb.

"What the...devil?" whispered past her lips.

Unable to move a muscle, she watched in morbid fascination as he hooked the sunglasses onto his hip pocket and strode toward the house—toward her. Sadie wouldn't have been able to summon a warning that he was trespassing had her life depended on just a simple two-letter word. The dogs growled while matching his steps, backing up until they were behind their master.

"Sadie." Lyle glanced at the shotgun as he reached up and removed his hat. "Expecting company?"

As if her heart had suddenly started to pump once more, kicking her brain into gear, fury blasted through her frozen muscles. "What do you want, Lyle McCaleb?" Somehow, despite the outrage roaring like a swollen river inside her, the words were frail and small. It still hurt, damn it, after all these years, to say his name out loud.

"Seeing as you didn't know I was coming, that couldn't be for me." He gave a nod toward her shotgun.

This could not be happening. Seven years he'd been gone. This was...this was... "I have nothing to say to you." She turned her back to him and walked away. Who did he think he was, showing up here like this after all this time? It was crazy. He was crazy!

"I know I'm the last person on this earth you want to see."

Her feet stopped when she wanted to keep going. To get inside the house and slam the door and dead-bolt it.

"We need to talk."

Sadie closed her eyes. Why was she standing here listening to anything he had to say? This was crazy all right. Crazy of her to hesitate like this. Hadn't she been a fool for him one time too many already?

"It's about your daddy."

She whipped around and glared at him but still couldn't find her voice. For Pete's sake, she hated the way her eyes drank in every single drop of him. His hair was as dark and silky as before. Those vivid blue eyes still made her want to sink into him, as if wading deep into the ocean with no care for how she'd stay afloat since she'd never learned to swim. He'd changed in other ways though. The cute boyish features had developed into rugged, handsome male assets. And in the face of all she had suffered because of him, he still made her body burn with need. With the primal urge to run into his arms.

Seeing him somehow made her momentarily forget those years of misery she'd endured because of something he had refused to give her seven years ago, and he damned sure wasn't here to give her his heart today.

She kicked the momentary weakness aside and grabbed back her good sense. "What about him?" she demanded. To her immense relief she sounded more like herself now. In charge, independent. Strong, ready to do battle.

"There's an investigation under way that I'm hoping is groundless." He flared those big hands that as a wild teenager she would have given anything to feel roving over her body. "I don't know if I can help him, but he's in way over his head. The only chance I've got of derailing the situation is with your help. I *need* your help."

Narrowing her gaze, she searched his face, tried her level best to look beyond the handsome features and see what he was hiding. He was hiding something. Didn't matter that it had been seven years. She knew Lyle McCaleb. He'd never been able to lie to her, even when she would have preferred his lies to the truth. He couldn't love her.

Whatever he wanted, he could forget it. Her heart had mended in time. She wasn't giving him a second shot at that kind of pain. "I hope you didn't drive all the way here from wherever you came from just for that."

"Houston."

If he'd sucker punched her, her physical reaction couldn't have been more debilitating. He'd been that close all this time? Gus had told her he'd moved to California, had a wife. Someone mature enough and smart enough to hang on to a man like him. A new rush of anger blasted her, obliterating the ache he'd resurrected with that one word. "Whatever. You wasted your time. Go away."

Before she could turn her back a second time and escape this surreal encounter, he opened his mouth again. "I was wrong not to call." He shook his head, stared at the ground a moment. "I was wrong about a lot of things."

Now she was really mad. "Let me tell you something else you're wrong about, McCaleb." She propped the barrel of her shotgun on her shoulder. "You're wrong if you think I give one damn about what kind of trouble my daddy might be in, because I don't." She amped up the go-to-hell glare in her eyes. "And you're dead wrong if you think for one second I care what you need."

Lyle watched, his heart somewhere in the vicinity of his throat, as she stamped up the steps and across the porch. She stormed into the house, slamming the door, without even a glance over her shoulder. The dogs stared after her, then turned to him in expectation.

That didn't exactly go the way he'd planned. Not even close. There was no denying that she did have every reason to hate him. He'd foolishly hoped that wasn't the case.

He blew out a breath and opted for plan B. Sit on the porch and wait. The dogs did the same, keeping their distance and eyeing him curiously but not bothering to bark. She wouldn't call the sheriff's office and have him escorted off her property. Not considering what he'd learned about the war going on between her and the rodeo kings around the county. Sheriff Cox was a good man as far as Lyle knew, but he held an elected position, and in this territory the rodeo kings ruled.

Lyle chuckled. Sadie Adele Gilmore had always been a hellion. In that respect she evidently hadn't changed one bit. She liked bucking the status quo, particularly when it involved the good old boys. She and her father had never really gotten along, not since she was old enough to have a mind of her own anyway. The best he recalled, she'd been damned independent since the age of six. His heart swelled a little more at the idea of what had been hidden from her all these years. He hated like hell to be the one to turn her life upside down like this, but he sure wasn't allowing anyone else to do the job. He owed her that much. He'd hurt her, but he'd made the only choice he could at the time. Nothing he said or did now would change that tragic fact, but he had to protect her.

He couldn't *not* protect her.

Her daddy wasn't going to like it. The last exchange between Gus and Lyle had been several degrees below amicable. The old man would be livid when he learned Lyle was back. The one thing Lyle could absolutely guarantee was that he wasn't walking away this time. For Gus or any other reason.

Wrestling aside his emotions, Lyle focused on what he'd come here to do. Whatever happened from this moment on was his responsibility. Whether she liked it or not. That part he'd just have to figure out. This battle between her and Gus had gone too far, if all he'd discovered was accurate. That was a whole different ball of wax and complicated an already dangerous situation. It pained him that she had been fighting a man like her daddy alone all this time. Lyle had left seven years ago when he should have stayed. He dropped his head. Staying hadn't been possible, no matter how he looked at the past. Things had been far too volatile. He'd had no choice but to leave.

By God, he was here now.

Sadie had a soft spot for animals, all of them. He surveyed the herd of furry critters lounging around his feet. Apparently she'd made it her life's mission to save every one she could, especially those involved with the rodeo that, for one reason or another, were neglected or otherwise abused. That decision had made a lot of folks unhappy around here, particularly Gus Gilmore. She'd gotten more than one, including her daddy, fined by the rodeo association for crossing the line when it came to the treatment of the animals they owned. Many times the incidents were mistakes or oversights, but others were intentional acts intended to ensure a crowd-pleasing performance. The latter could prove hazardous to the person or persons who got in the way.

Lyle stared at his hat, turning it in his hands as if an answer could be pulled from there, but there was no easy answer. Sadie's troubles with the ranchers were the least of her problems right now. Making her understand that reality without revealing too much too soon would be the hardest part. Her cooperation was absolutely essential, but he despised keeping anything from her for any reason.

The fact was he couldn't protect her fully if she didn't cooperate. The situation presented a precarious balancing act. The last thing he wanted to do was hurt her again. Or to let anyone else hurt her. Unfortunately, whatever happened, protecting her from the shocking truth was not possible. She had to know all of it, eventually.

Movement beyond the end of the house caught his eye. He watched her march out to the barn, her shotgun still propped on her shoulder. She'd captured her long, silky blond hair into a haphazard ponytail that hung to the middle of her back. She'd worn it that way for as long as he could remember. The scrap of leather she used to tie it back always ended up barely clasping that gorgeous mane below her shoulders, as if she didn't possess the patience to bother with securing it adequately at the nape of her neck. Her grandmother had scolded her about never staying still long enough to properly brush her hair, much less prepare a suitable ponytail. The memory of running his fingers through her hair warred with the logic required to stay on track. He banished those snippets of lost moments the same way he'd been doing for the past seven years.

The dogs, one by one, got up and moseyed out to the barn to see what their master was up to. Lyle stood, settled his hat into place, and followed. Her soft voice stopped him at the wide-open barn doors. She'd set her shotgun aside and filled a bucket with feed. One by one she served the stabled animals. Chatted softly with each one and gave the old horses a scratch behind the ears. When she'd finished she walked right past Lyle and released all but one horse into the pasture.

The barn and the house were a little run-down. In all likelihood there was fencing that needed mending. Had she been trying to handle this place all alone the better part of the time? The thought made his gut clench. Damn Gus Gilmore. Lyle shook his head. Damn *him*. She hadn't deserved the raw deal she'd gotten from him anymore than from her daddy.

Sadie made eye contact with him as she strode back to the front of the barn. "You haven't left yet?" Her arms went over her chest as her chin lifted in challenge.

"I'm afraid leaving isn't an option."

"You're something." She shook her head, fury blazing in those green eyes her grandmother had sworn came from her Irish roots. Lyle knew different. Sadie was the only one of the Barker girls who had her biological mother's green eyes. "You take off, stay gone for seven years and now you show up needing *my* help. I don't know what you've been smoking, but I think you'd better find some place to clear your head."

"Like I said before—" he folded his arms over his chest, matching her stance and, partly, to keep from grabbing her and shaking her or worse, kissing the hell out of her "—I was wrong."

"Like *you* also said," she echoed, "you were wrong about a lot of things, but that changes nothing."

"I really need your help, Sadie. This isn't just about Gus."

A frown furrowed her soft brow. Damn, she looked good in those work-worn jeans and that pink button-up shirt that hugged her body the way he had dreamed of doing for too many years to count.

"All right, I'll bite. What's this about then?"

At least her question was a step in the right direction. "The trouble involves you, too."

She rolled her eyes and made a sound of disbelief. "I don't believe you. Besides, I'm always in trouble. What's new?"

"This could get ugly fast." Urgency nudged him. "There's no time to say what I need to say the polite way." Might as well spit it out. "I've been sent here to protect you 24/7, until this is over."

He'd expected her to get her shotgun, maybe rant at him a little more, and attempt running him off. He was prepared for that kind of reaction. He wasn't set for her laughter. The sound burst out of her. "You really are out of your mind, Lyle McCaleb. You should go now, before I lose my sense of humor."

He had one last ace up his sleeve. "You think you're unhappy to see me." He chuckled. "Imagine how Gus will feel when he finds out I'm back." Lyle grinned, couldn't help himself. "He's really going to hit the roof. You know how much he hates me. I'll bet word has already climbed its way up to that pedestal he lives on."

That gave her pause and maybe a little anticipatory pleasure. It flashed like a neon sign across her pretty face. "I'm not saying you can stay or even that I believe anything you're saying," she countered, but her resolve had weakened ever so slightly. He heard it in her voice. "But I'll hear you out and then I'll make my decision."

"Rumor has it you're out here all by yourself." That worried him the most.

Anger darkened the features he knew by heart, yanking the step he'd gained right out from under his feet. "I don't appreciate you checking up on me. I'm perfectly capable of taking care of myself."

"I'm just doing my job, Sadie. My orders are to make sure you're protected. To do that I have to know what I'm up against."

Suspicion made an appearance amid the other emotions visibly tugging at her. "Who sent you here? You working for the law again? I thought you went off to be some hotshot security specialist."

The Colby Agency never failed its clients, particularly not where their safety was concerned. Yes, he was here representing those high standards. He supposed one could reason that he was operating under Colby Law. "The answer's complicated, Sadie. There's no simple way to explain it." He didn't dare say more, much less breathe. All he needed was half a chance to protect her with her cooperation…to do right by her this time.

"Well." She dropped her arms to her sides, hooked her right thumb in a belt loop and pursed those perfect bow lips the way she had at fifteen. The image made him ache to trace those sweet lips with his fingers, then with his lips. "You're right about one thing. Gus ran off all my help and there is a lot of work to be done. I can't deny your conclusions there."

"It's been a while." He glanced around, noting the repairs that immediately jumped out at him, such as the barn's old tin roof. It could use a little TLC. He shrugged. "Just like riding a bicycle. Point me in a starting direction and I'll get back in the swing of things faster than old Dare Devil used to toss his riders." He'd noticed the old champion among those under her care. Dare Devil was the only one she hadn't let out to roam in the pasture. Had to be a reason for that. Gus, he suspected. And more trouble.

Something wicked glittered in her eyes as she pointed up to the barn roof. "The extension ladder's in the toolshed. You'll find anything else you need there, too. Long as you stay busy and out of my way. You've got a deal. *For the day.*"

Lyle surveyed the first step toward gaining her co-operation if not her trust, three stories up at the very least. Nothing he hadn't done before.

Sadie headed back into the barn. "Come supper," she called back at him, "I'll expect some answers, and then you'll have my final decision."

Lyle pointed his boots in the direction of the tool-shed. If it kept her alive, he could walk a tightrope all the way across Texas.

If he was lucky, he would live through the experience.

Chapter Four

Five Hills Apartments, 2:00 p.m.

What now? What now?

It wasn't supposed to happen this way. She had a plan, a carefully laid plan. This could ruin everything! She paced the small studio apartment. Back and forth, back and forth. Perhaps the problem was only temporary.

At the window, Clare Barker peeked through the slats of the yellowed blinds covering her one portal to the outside world. The car was still there. Oh, no, no, no. Who was this man watching her? The warden had relished telling her that as soon as she was delivered to this location she was on her own. She knew what he wanted—he wanted some vigilante to carry out the justice the whole world believed had been denied by an appeals court. Her lips tightened. But this man had not gone away. He was not supposed to be here! He changed everything.

Her fingers knotted together as the worry rose in her throat once more, the taste as bitter as yesterday's coffee dregs. *He* had sent this man to kill her. She knew it! She just knew it. It was the only way to stop her, that was for sure. He would know his options were limited. Had he prepared so well?

Rage boiled in her belly. But he would fail. The fury stretched her lips into a knowing smile. *He would fail.*

More than twenty years she had planned this moment. *He* would pay for what he had done to her. No force on earth could stop her without sending her to hell first.

Time was her most fierce enemy. There was no room for distractions. Clare turned away from the window. Her reflection in the mirror mounted to the bathroom door of her efficiency apartment snared her attention. She was old now. The lines of her frown were deep and ugly. Her hair more gray than the blond it had once been. She touched the shaggy ends she had bobbed off to her ears. No use making it easy for anyone looking for her. She studied the hollows beneath her eyes and the crow's feet nothing short of a face-lift would remedy. All those years within those stark, punishing walls had stolen her youth, her beauty. She had nothing left, save for this long-awaited final act of retribution.

Clare went to the tattered sofa, where her most prized possessions were arranged like a shrine. She lit the small candle on the end table and dropped to her knees. Confident in her ability to overcome all blockades thrown in her path, she studied the photos lined up against the back of the worn cushions. Each one would soon know the truth. Each one would feel her pain and finally understand what only a mother who had sacrificed so much could.

And before they answered to their maker for their sins, each one would realize that it had never been *what if* wicked old Clare won one of her many appeals. It had always been simply a matter of time.

There was no escaping destiny.

Clare bowed her head and began to pray. She prayed for strength, for courage to stay her course. Once it was done, she cared little what happened to her.

She lifted her gaze to the photos worn by time and the caress of her fingers. Mommy was here now. The waiting and wondering would soon be over.

Chapter Five

Sadie washed up and tossed the hand towel aside. What was she doing? Her reflection didn't give her the answer she wanted to see. All she saw in the mirror was a woman who still wanted the only man she'd ever loved. The man who'd left her with painful words that rang in her ears to this day.

I can't do this, Sadie. You're just a kid. I don't have time for games.

Anger and hurt—yes, hurt—twisted her heart. He'd left and she'd cried herself to sleep every night for months. What the hell was she doing allowing him to worm his way back into her life for any reason? The answer resonated in her brain as clearly as the last words he'd uttered to her all those years ago. Despite their miserable history, a tiny piece of her wanted to believe that it could be different now. Yeah, he was still six years older than her, but she was twenty-two—soon to be twenty-three—a lifetime away from fifteen.

Did that really change anything? Of course not. Just because he was here to do a job didn't mean he felt any different today than he had seven years ago. Did she?

She'd thought she was way over Lyle McCaleb ages ago, but apparently she'd been lying to herself.

As angry and disgusted as she was with her own stupidity and his audacity, she might as well get this over with. Her excuses for hanging out in the bathroom had run out. Time to face the reality of this bizarre turn of events and get some answers from the man.

Taking a big breath, she opened the door and stalled. What was that smell? Fried potatoes? She sniffed the air like a beagle on the scent of a rabbit. Corn bread? Her mouth watered as much at the memory of her grandmother's cooking the scents evoked as at the delicious smells themselves wafting from her kitchen right now.

Lyle cooking? No way. Had Walley, the last employee to leave her high and dry and the only one who could cook, come crawling back? Not likely. He was far too afraid of Gus. She wandered to the kitchen, pausing in the doorway to get the lay of the land. No Walley in sight. Hat hanging on a kitchen chair, a red-and-white striped dish towel slung over one broad shoulder, Lyle McCaleb stirred what she presumed to be the potatoes revving her appetite. Sadie leaned against the door frame, too shocked to speak or maybe too curious to risk interrupting. This was a side of Lyle she had never seen. Then again, the fact that their every encounter before had been on the sly might have something to do with that.

He checked the oven, allowing more of that heavenly aroma of fresh-baked corn bread to sift through the air. Still apparently oblivious to her presence, he rummaged through the slim pickings of her supplies, opening one cupboard after the other, and came up with a can she recognized as beans she'd forgotten was there. Probably some of her grandmother's left-over supplies. While the electric can opener whined with the effort of releasing the contents of the can, her attention somehow got trapped on Lyle's backside, specifically the fit of his jeans. He'd been handsome and nicely built before, but now he was…she licked her lips…just plain hot. As if her traitorous body needed to prove the theory, heat simmered through her limbs, settling in that place she had ignored for way too long.

Stop, Sadie. Lyle was here. Out of the blue. She'd tried to reason out his explanation for showing up, but it didn't add up. As far as she knew, Gus wasn't doing anything differently than he'd done for years. Why would the authorities be interested in him now? Just because he was a greedy, ruthless SOB didn't make him a criminal. Just a heartless bastard who happened to be her father, unfortunately. Lyle had suggested her name had been mentioned in whatever trouble was brewing. That was nothing new. She spent most of her time on somebody's horse manure list and ignoring the sheriff's stern warnings.

No. She straightened and steeled herself for a fight. This excuse of his for requesting her cooperation didn't hold water. She wouldn't accuse him of lying, but he was most definitely hedging the truth. As curious as she was about him and what he'd been up to the past seven years, everyone knew that curiosity killed the cat.

"Looks like you've picked up a few new skills while you've been away." She crossed her arms over her chest and strolled over to the stove. Yep, fried potatoes. Browned to a nice crisp. Her stomach rumbled.

She hadn't eaten anything that fit into the home-cooked category in ages. Eggs didn't count unless they were a part of a casserole or other dish. Walley had been the one to dare to stock fresh vegetables. After he'd gone, they'd all ended up horse treats before going bad. Except for the potatoes. She'd been known to pop one in the microwave and wait for the explosion indicating it was done.

"When you live alone—" Lyle wiped his hands on the towel then deposited it on the counter "—you learn to fend for yourself."

Well, well. It appeared things hadn't worked out with the other woman. She had noted there was no ring on the appropriate finger. No rings at all, as a matter of fact. Was that glee flittering around in her tummy or just more hunger pangs? *Get to the point, girl.* If she was nice she would start by telling him how much she appreciated the work he'd accomplished on the barn roof, but she wasn't feeling too nice right now. "We have to talk."

He bent down and pulled the bread from the oven. Her knees practically went weak with desire—only this time it was about the way that fresh, hot corn bread smelled. She was starving! He flipped the iron skillet and a perfect, round cake of bread settled on the plate. Hers never came out looking like that. She generally had to scrape it out of the skillet in a crumbled mess.

"How about we eat first?" He emptied the beans into a pan. "Five minutes and I'll be good to go here." He flaunted one of those sexy smiles that came naturally to him. "Milk sounds good. You could pour us a tall glass and set the table."

Milk? What was she, fifteen again? She squared her

shoulders. "I have beer." She hoped she had beer. And he could set the table himself.

He gave the beans a stir. "None for me. I'll stick with the milk."

For some reason his declining ticked her off. "That's right, you're working."

He gave her another of those cute-as-hell smiles. "What kind of bodyguard would I be if I allowed my senses to be dulled on the job?"

Bodyguard? She started to challenge the idea, but the thought drifted away as she got lost visually measuring those broad shoulders. She really needed to get out more. It took some effort and a mental knock upside the head to redirect her attention to ferreting out the beer she hoped she had. Sadie opened the door of the fridge her grandmother had bought several decades before she was born and studied the meager contents. Milk, eggs, half a stick of butter. One beer lying on its side way in the back. Thank goodness. She wasn't really a beer drinker, but if she'd ever needed one it was now. Three or four might have better served the purpose of escape from this weird situation.

She popped the top while Lyle served up the goods he'd prepared. Her stomach demanded that she follow his suggestion and eat first. Fine. She dragged out a chair and dropped into it. They would talk after dinner. Lyle placed a plate laden with potatoes, beans and corn bread in front of her, along with a fork and a napkin. A cloth napkin. Sadie frowned. "Where—?"

"In the middle drawer of the buffet in the dining room." He placed the same on his side of the table. "You've got napkins and tablecloths in several patterns and colors."

She'd lived in this house going on two years and didn't have a clue where those napkins were stored. She fingered the yellow one he'd chosen. Sniffed it, the aroma of cedar-lined drawers taking her back. Her grandmother had saved her best cloth napkins for special occasions, but the solid-colored ones like this had been on the table every day. How had she forgotten that? Sadie shook off the memories and placed the napkin in her lap.

Lyle poured himself a glass of milk and downed half of it before he reached the table. Sadie looked away. The way his throat moved as he drank or the way he licked his lips afterward shouldn't bother her. He was the enemy. Funny, it seemed all the men in her life were enemies of one sort or the other. Didn't say much for her relationship skills. Or her choices in associates.

A long swallow of beer didn't make her feel any less flustered. Maybe another would do the trick. By the time she settled the can on the table it was more than half-empty. Reluctantly, she picked up her fork. She was starving but she detested the idea of him seeing he'd done good. And man, had he done good. The potatoes were crispy on the outside and soft on the inside. And the bread was moist with a firm, rich crust. How the heck did he know how to do this?

Sadie blocked out all else and devoured the meal. She swallowed the last bite of bread and barely stifled a satisfied moan. Using the cloth napkin she was glad he'd found, she dabbed her lips, all the while considering seconds. That feeling of being watched scrambled across her skin. She looked up to find him staring at her. She blinked. Her fingers found and curled around the half empty can of beer. She finished it off to prevent having to speak or maintain eye contact. Maybe she hadn't kept all those appreciative moans to herself.

Lyle ate more slowly than she and he was nowhere near finished. Sadie worked hard at waiting him out but she couldn't do it. Watching his lips wrap around the fork was too much. She pushed back her chair and stood. "I'll clean up." He started to argue but she waved him off and moved on. As badly as she wanted to know the details of his unexpected appearance, she couldn't talk right now.

She'd fed the dogs, stored the leftovers, washed the cookware and her plate and utensils by the time he arrived at her side, his plate and fork in hand. Before he could strike up a conversation—the one she'd come in here to have and then chickened out—she thrust the hand towel at him. "Wipe down the table."

Rushing to finish first, she washed the last plate, rinsed her hands, dried them on her jeans and got out of there. Out of the house—the house that was suddenly filled with him and his hot body and wondrous new talents. Pretending seven years ago hadn't happened was mentally beyond her at the moment, yet somehow her body hadn't gotten the message. Sadie collapsed in the old wicker rocker that badly needed a fresh coat of white paint and pulled her knees up to her chest. Her dogs stretched out around her, full and happy.

For the first time in her life she felt good about herself and what she was accomplishing. Why did he have to show up now and stir around all those old feelings of inadequacy? She'd finally moved on with her life. What did fate have against her? Was it too much to ask for a small reprieve between dramatic episodes?

The screen door grumbled as he pushed it open and

joined her on the porch. He walked over to the chair right next to her and lowered his tall frame there. As much as she recognized that there were many things that needed to be said, she didn't want to talk. Definitely didn't want to hear his voice or smell that earthy male scent of his. His presence was driving her nuts. The longer he was here, the more jittery she got. Why couldn't she shut out all that stimuli and pretend it didn't matter?

Because she was weak when it came to him, and she hated weakness.

"I was wrong not to call."

He didn't look at her as he said the words. Not that she looked at him either, except a sneak peek from the corner of her eyes, but she wasn't the one seemingly trying to make the past right. "You said that already." Twice.

"When it became clear that this case involved you," he went on, still staring off across the land that had been in the Gilmore family for six generations, "I asked myself if coming here was the right thing to do or if it would be best to let another, more objective investigator take over."

The idea shouldn't have unsettled her. But like everything else about him, it did. "Why didn't you?" She resisted looking at him, but failed. His profile was exactly as she remembered. A little more chiseled and defined. The one night they had spent together in each other's arms, she'd lain awake and watched him breathe. He'd refused to make love to her, kept telling her it would be wrong. She was too young. The memory hurt her chest. The next day she had pleaded with him to stay. He'd left anyway, breaking her heart into a thousand pieces.

He'd better have a damned good reason for barging back into her life now. Whatever the reason, she wanted the whole truth. She willed him to meet her gaze so she could confirm the words he intended to say. As difficult as being this close was, she wasn't letting him take the easy way out. Sadie Gilmore used her brain for guidance more often than her heart these days.

Finally, he surrendered his full attention to her. "I couldn't risk that someone else might fail to protect you the way I would."

There it was—that shiver his voice had always set off deep inside her when they were this close. "I can protect myself," she argued for all the good it would do. He was as stubborn as she was. "I've been doing it for quite some time now. Maybe you hadn't noticed." Sadie held up her hands stop-sign fashion. "Wait, that's right. You weren't here." Good grief, could she wave her woman-scorned flag any more vigorously? She should be handling this better. No, she shouldn't be talking to him at all. He was the one with the explaining to do. *Stay calm. Keep your mouth shut.*

He exhaled a frustrated breath. "I don't doubt your ability to take care of yourself, Sadie. Not for a minute." He twisted in the chair, putting himself face-to-face with her. "You've done a damned good job. I admire what you've accomplished. But you have to trust me when I say you can't do this alone. This is different from any of the troubles you've faced head-on in the past. You need my help."

She searched his eyes, fear trickling into her chest.

The reality of the situation abruptly sank past the bitterness and resentment she'd used as a defense against him and his memory all this time. Whatever he hadn't told her, she suddenly knew without doubt it was bad. Really bad. His eyes told the story his words hadn't quite given her yet. That was why he was here. He hadn't finally returned to make amends. Gus was in big trouble. Her, too, apparently.

"That's ridiculous. What could possibly be so terrible?" Her voice trembled with that blasted fear she couldn't dismiss and a tad of silly disappointment. She loathed showing him that infernal weakness. She hated even more that she so desperately wanted to lean on him. Sadie Gilmore, the girl who thought she could take on the world. How could he still possess the power to make her feel needy when there wasn't a man in this county who could even come close?

Lyle hesitated. He had to choose his words and his actions carefully. The photo album was in the truck. He could show it to her. Get it all out in the open and shatter her world in one fell swoop. But that would be taking a major risk. The shock would make her irrational, and cooperation would go out the window. He needed her complete cooperation in order to protect her from this threat. There were steps that needed to be taken. Confirmation that Sadie really was Sarah, the same for the other women pointed to as allegedly being the Barkers' missing, presumed-dead children. Two of the Colby Agency's best were already in place with the middle and older daughters.

"More than twenty years ago," he began the cover story he'd decided upon, "a couple in Granger were arrested for a series of murders. The Barkers, Raymond and Clare." He watched for any recognition in her eyes before continuing. If she remembered the murders he saw no indication in her expression. She'd been just a toddler at the time. "Two days ago Clare Barker was released after winning an appeal that reversed her conviction. There are those who believe she should not have been released and that she poses a threat to anyone she may have had association with before her arrest."

"What does that have to do with me or Gus?"

Now for the sticky part. "That's where things get a little murky. We don't have a definitive link between your father and Clare Barker, but there is some indication that he may be on her list of former associates and, as I said, that makes him and his family a target. Particularly his family. Generally, in these cases, the family is used to ensure the desired outcome."

The beginnings of true fear clouded her face. "If it's Gus's name on her list, then it's my father who needs protection. The idea that she might come after me is just speculation."

"Considering the personal security he surrounds himself with, we felt you were the most accessible target. If Gus has something or knows something that Barker wants, you would be the fastest way to pressure him for cooperation."

"Like he cares what happens to me." Sadie made a sound of disbelief, even though his theory made an undeniable sense that showed in her eyes. "He'd like nothing more than to get me out of the way."

"I think you know that isn't true. The two of you

have your differences, but you're still his only child."
At least legally. Damn, this wasn't going to be easy.

"So this threat is real." She hesitated. "The real
reason you came back."

The disappointment in her voice, in her eyes was
impossible to miss. The last thing he wanted to do
was hurt her again, and apparently he'd already done
that. "The threat is real. I am here to protect you, that's
true. But I should have come back a long time ago.
It shouldn't have taken something like this." He had
to look away. "The way I left things was wrong and
there's no excuse for that."

"Well." She dropped her feet to the floor and stood,
avoiding eye contact. "I have chores."

He got up, blocked her escape. "I need to know I can
count on your cooperation, at least for a little while.
Until we know what Clare's intentions are."

"I have to think about this. You can stay the night
in the barn or in your truck." She met his gaze then,
anger simmering in hers. "I'll give you my decision
tomorrow."

At least he had the night. That was a beginning.

Sadie stopped at the bottom of the steps and turned
back to him. "Does Gus know about this?"

More dicey territory. "The fewer people who know,
the less likely the waters will be muddied. You know
Gus, he'll have his own security folks trying to track
down Barker. That would be a mistake. It's imperative
that we catch her in the act so that she can be properly
prosecuted. Otherwise she may get away with more
heinous crimes." Like Janet Tolliver's murder. He kept
that to himself for now. "There's a lot we haven't nailed
down yet. Revealing our hand too soon could send this

woman into hiding, and then you might never be safe again."

Sadie started for the barn once more. "What can I do to help?" he called after her. When she glanced back at him, he added, "With the rest of the chores."

She shook her head. "I've got this."

One step forward, two steps back. He'd expected shaky ground. He just hoped the ground didn't crack open and swallow him up before this case was solved.

Simon had called with an update on Janet Tolliver's great-niece. Nothing appeared missing from the house as best she could determine. Her aunt had no safe-deposit boxes and no known attorneys. For some reason, Tolliver had decided to move back to the home that had belonged to her own aunt a few months back. She'd told her niece it was the one place she'd always felt at peace. The niece had nothing more to offer. Whatever else Tolliver knew, that information had died with her.

The rumble of engines dragged Lyle from those troubling thoughts. With the dust flying it was difficult to make out how many vehicles were roaring toward Sadie's house, but he estimated three. The first, then the second and third skidded to a halt not twenty feet from the porch. He recognized the driver of the first vehicle before the man launched out the door, rifle in hand.

Gus Gilmore.

The man was obviously losing his edge. Lyle had anticipated an appearance hours ago. Word traveled fast to men like Gilmore. Lyle took his time walking out to meet him. No need to hurry into trouble. From beneath the porch, Sadie's herd of dogs yapped that strange harmony of high-pitched Chihuahua and deep, booming Lab.

"What the hell are you doing here?" Gus stopped in front of his truck, four of his cohorts lined up around him. Lyle recognized only one—celebrity bronc rider Billy Sizemore. He'd been a cocky bastard before. Lyle doubted that caveman flaw had evolved much.

"Hello to you, too, Gus. It's been a while." Lyle braced his hands on his hips. His weapon was secured in his truck. As smart-mouthed and bullish as these men wanted to appear, Lyle wasn't afraid of one or all. It took more than mere guts to shoot an unarmed man. These bozos were lacking in that department, along with a few others, like morals.

"I warned you once before," Gus threatened. "You better stay away from my little girl."

Lyle glanced toward the barn, hoped Sadie stayed put. "Your little girl is a grown woman now. She can make decisions for herself. Word is, she doesn't take orders from you any more than I intend to."

Sizemore started forward. Gus stopped him with an uplifted hand. "I've kept up with you, McCaleb. Just because you work for some fancy P.I. agency doesn't make you any better than the green deputy you were before." His face tightened with his building rage. "I don't know what you're doing back here, but I will find out. Meanwhile, you'd better watch your back."

The unmistakable racking of a shotgun punctuated his warning. "Lyle is my guest."

Lyle's gaze swung to his right. *Sadie.* The woman had a way of sneaking up on a man. Not a one of the bunch had heard her approach. She stood a few feet away, her shotgun readied for use. If she spilled the beans…

"You go on in the house, Sadie," her daddy ordered. "This is between me and him. The fact that he's standing here proves you don't have a lick of sense, much less any pride."

Lyle resisted the urge to grin. Gus should have known better than to take that approach. Lyle braced for the inevitable explosion.

Sadie, shotgun still positioned and ready for firing, walked right up to her daddy. "This is my property, in case you've forgotten, Gus Gilmore. Now take your low-down friends and get off my ranch."

Gus moved closer to her, allowing the muzzle to burrow into his chest. Lyle held his protective instincts in check. Any move he made would escalate this scene and wouldn't have a good ending.

"I ran him out of town once," Gus reminded her. "I'll do it again. And that horse you stole from me, I will get him back, one way or another."

"You'll try," she countered fearlessly. "But I bought him fair and square. The sheriff already told you the papers were good. So don't waste your time, old man. That horse is done, just like you."

Gus glared at her another five seconds before turning back to Lyle. "You heed what I say, boy. Or you'll wish you had. Your connections back in Houston don't carry any weight here. This is my county."

Lyle didn't rise to the bait. He held his temper and let Gus and his minions go on their way. There would be a day when he and that old bastard resolved their differences. Just not today.

When the dust had settled, he considered the woman

caught up in all this turmoil. How did she deal with that man on a regular basis? Living right next door, though hundreds of acres separated Gus's mansion from her modest home, had to be a real pain in the butt.

"You okay?" He noted the slightest tremor in her arms.

"Course." Sadie lowered the business end of her gun. "But he'll be back." She shook her head. "Once he gets his teeth into something he never lets go."

Now Lyle understood why Sadie hadn't permitted Dare Devil to roam the pasture with the other horses. "What's the deal with Dare Devil?"

"His rodeo days are done." She dusted the front of her shirt, removing the hay that had stuck there during her work in the barn. "Gus had him parading around in all kinds of absurd trick shows. Dare Devil couldn't take it. A friend of mine who works for Gus loaded him up with the horses for auction and I bought him. Gus can't prove I tricked him. The only thing he can prove is a series of mistakes that more than one of his employees made. Even the sheriff had to agree with me." She pointed a knowing look in Lyle's direction. "Trust me, that was a first."

Prior to his arrival, Lyle had discovered there was some frivolous trouble between her and her daddy, but this felt more complicated than he'd been led to believe. As much as he disliked Gus, he couldn't see him hurting his daughter physically. But then, she wasn't his daughter. Had his own mother's choosing Sadie as her heir over him been the last straw? If so, why hadn't he shattered Sadie's world by telling her that truth? "Doesn't sound like he's ready to let it go," Lyle suggested.

"That's his problem." Sadie climbed the porch steps. "I'll be sleeping in the barn tonight. Sleep where you want."

Since the house wasn't nearly close enough to the barn to suit him, he'd be sleeping in the barn, too. "I figure there's plenty of room for both of us out there."

Sadie glanced back at him, opened her mouth to say something then snapped it shut. Halfway across the porch, she mumbled, "Suit yourself."

He planned to. The air was too thick with the trouble brewing to let her too far out of his reach. He just had to remember that every square inch of that gorgeous little body of hers was off-limits. There would be no finishing what they'd started that final night seven years ago. She deserved better.

Keeping her safe was the easy part, as long as he maintained his focus. It was the part that came after that tore him up inside. If there was any way in the world he could protect her from what was coming he would...but there wasn't.

The only thing he could do was keep her safe until the imminent physical threat passed. He couldn't shield her from the rest. Not without kidnapping her and disappearing. But then, someone had already done that once, and look how that effort turned out.

Clare Barker wanted her girls back. Whether to finish the job her husband didn't complete or for a happy reunion, Lyle couldn't say just yet. But she wanted something, and the only side of the story they had was her husband's.

Between Lucas Camp watching Clare and two of the agency's researchers digging through the Princess

Killer case files, they had to piece together the truth soon. For Sadie's sake. As well as the others.

For now, anyone who tried to get to Sadie—Clare Barker or Gus Gilmore included—would have to go through Lyle.

Chapter Six

May 22, 2:00 a.m.

Sadie stirred from the dreams plaguing her sleep. She swiped at her nose and frowned. The sweet scent of hay sifted into her groggy senses. Scrubbing her face with the back of her hand, she sat up. It was dark. Darker than when she'd bedded down in the vacant stall closest to Dare Devil.

What happened to the light she'd left on in the tack room? She felt for the shotgun lying next to her, untangled herself from the blanket and stumbled to her feet. A low sound brushed her awareness. She froze.

Listening for the faint rasp to come again, she maneuvered her way out of the stall by touch. The barn doors were closed, blocking out the glow from the moon and stars. She stilled a second time and listened. Scratching? Whimpering?

The dogs.

Bewildered, Sadie moved slowly along the corridor between the stalls. One of the horses shuffled, likely awakened by the same noise that had dragged her back to consciousness. She checked each stall she passed, sliding a calming hand over the animal's forehead. The urge to call out to the dogs burgeoned in her throat, but she preferred not to give her position away if trouble was lurking around outside.

Damn that Billy Sizemore. If he'd come back to try to scare her, she might just shoot his sorry butt this time.

Sadie sensed the stall closest to the big entry doors was empty before she felt around on the fresh haystack and found Lyle's abandoned blanket. Where the hell was he? It wasn't enough that he'd invaded her dreams. He had to be missing in action now that she might actually need him?

That was just like a man. All talk and no action of the right kind. When had honor become obsolete?

At the doors, she crouched down to calm the mutts. She whispered softly to them and gave each a soothing back rub. Allowing them outside would be a bad idea, seeing as the three were all bark and no bite whatsoever. Ushering them into the stall with Lyle's blanket would be futile. They'd only follow her right back to the doors.

What she actually needed was a vantage point with a view to assess the situation before barging out those doors anyway. She glanced around the dark barn then looked up, and a smile slid across her lips. Of course. *The loft.*

Slipping back to the center of the barn as quietly as possible with three dogs on her heels, she listened for any sound coming from beyond the old batten-and-board walls of the barn. Satisfied that all was quiet for the moment, she climbed the ladder to the hayloft. The loft door at the front of the barn that provided access for loading hay was open, allowing enough light for her to make her way there without tripping over any misplaced bales. She surveyed the grounds between the house and the barn. If anyone, including Lyle, was out there, they were well hidden. The only vehicle was her old truck and his shiny new one. No lights in the house.

Where the heck was he?

Sadie heaved a sigh. The man had her on edge. He was probably out there taking care of necessary business and she was in here worried about intruders and *him*.

"Ridiculous, Sadie," she muttered.

Picking her way back to the handmade ladder, she cursed herself for being such an idiot. Why had she let him stay? His explanations for his sudden appearance after all this time were far too vague. If he couldn't tell her exactly why he was here, why was *she* assuming he was on the up-and-up? She stepped off the final rung and walked back to her makeshift bed.

If she were honest with herself about her own motives, she would have to confess that she was curious, hazardous to her health or not, about him. Still had a crazy attraction to him. And she loved that his presence drove Gus nuts. None of those were good reasons for this situation. She lay back on her blanket. Then again, who said she had to have a good reason? The tightening sensation in her chest warned that the wrong reason could set her up for more of the heartache that still twisted her up into knots from time to time.

The distant sound of splintering wood fractured the silence. Gator, Frisco and Abigail burst into unharmonious barking. Sadie shot to her feet, shotgun in hand, and was at the barn doors before her brain had completed an inventory of the possible sources of the racket. Grabbing back control in the nick of time before she burst out of the barn, she eased one door open just far enough to scan the darkness. Still no lights on in the house. The two vehicles hadn't moved. No one swaggering about. Where in blazes was Lyle?

Squeezing out that same narrow crack, she pushed the door back into place before the dogs could hurtle out after her. The big pecan tree was her first destination, the disabled tractor next, then the toolshed and the outhouse as she crept closer to the house. She stilled, listened hard to determine the source of what sounded like distant thudding or pounding. *Thump, thump, thump.* The sound grew faster. Someone was running…in the woods that stretched out from the edge of her side yard all the way to the road.

Sadie summoned her courage and sprinted to the back corner of the house. She flattened against the peeling clapboard siding. The hurried footsteps had stopped…but there was a different activity now. Thrashing, maybe. The distinct splat of flesh slamming against flesh smacked the air. *Fighting.*

Her movements painstakingly slow, she rounded the corner of the house and moved toward the trees beyond the clothesline. The sound of running started again, accompanied by the crash of underbrush being disturbed.

Enough with the tiptoeing around. She couldn't see a damned thing, but this was her ranch and she intended to protect what belonged to her, especially the animals. Heart pumping hard, propelling the adrenaline-infused blood through her veins, Sadie dashed across the backyard and into the acres of woods that separated her house from the road.

Gunfire split the air.

She hit the ground, knocked the breath out of her. A third shot, then a fourth.

Oh, damn.

Staying in a low crouch, she scrambled forward. Fear pressed in on her. Did Lyle even have a gun? She hadn't seen one. Who knew? He could have anything stashed in that truck. Surely Gus and his men had not stooped to this level.

The ensuing hush had her pushing back to her feet and moving forward more quickly. Damn it, if Lyle was lying out here bleeding somewhere...

A trig snapped.

She froze. Leveled her aim in the direction from which the crack had resonated.

Close. That was really close. Her finger readied on the trigger. Her heart quieted, allowing complete focus. Someone was coming straight at her.

"Sadie, it's me."

Her heart dropped all the way to her bare feet. "What in the hell is going on, Lyle?"

"Let's get back to the house."

The fingers of one hand curled around her arm, and for a whole second she felt helpless and her knees went all rubbery. He lugged her back in the direction of the house, mumbling something about hurrying.

Reason abruptly slapped her in the face and she stalled, yanked against his hold. "What the hell is going on?" she repeated. "I am not a child. Stop treating me like one!"

"We're not safe out here like this," he urged in that deep voice that possessed the power to make her tremble. "Let's get inside first."

Furious for the wrong reason and just a little dazed, she trudged and stumbled alongside him, part of her attention on their backs even as they moved forward. Who had he chased off? Had someone broken into the house? Why hadn't he awakened her before he left the barn? It was her house!

Why was it men always thought they could boss her around? She was a grown woman and she was smart. There wasn't a damned thing in this world that she couldn't handle just as well as any man, including the shotgun she carried.

Lyle shoved the back door aside and hauled her into the kitchen. She staggered to a stop. "What…in the world?" The back door was hanging on only one hinge. The knob and locking mechanism as best she could tell hung slightly askew from their standard position. Who kicked her door in? Or out? Even the frame was no longer square and plumb.

He set her aside and proceeded to lift the door back into its damaged frame. Wood scrubbed against wood. "You got a hammer and some nails in the house?"

Her mind reeled with questions and conclusions, and her heart fluttered with the evaporating bewilderment and no shortage of fear. She wrestled it back the best she could and bobbed her head up and down. "I'll round them up."

Sadie flipped on the overhead light and gasped. The kitchen table was overturned, a couple of chairs had gone down with it. Her grandmother's antique stoneware sugar bowl lay in shards on the floor. Oh my God! Someone had been in her house! Her fear and confusion morphed into fury.

"Lock the front door and bring me those tools."

The stern order prompted her from the churning emotions making her feel disoriented. That was the first time she got a look at Lyle in the light. He was bleeding! "You're hurt!"

"It's just a scratch."

Closer inspection confirmed his typical male proclamation. "We need to clean it. At least."

He waved her off. "We'll deal with that when we're secure."

Secure. Did he think trouble was still out there? "Fine." That was just like a man. He could be bleeding out with the enemy bearing down on him and he'd swear he was good to go before he'd permit a glimmer of weakness. And he'd leave her in the dark about the trouble as long as possible. She locked the front door and stalled. Why was her door unlocked? She expressly remembered locking it before going to the barn for the night.

Frustrated and mad as hell, she stamped back to the kitchen in search of the tools. Where had she put them? She'd moved a painting in her room, then…now she remembered. The antique Hoosier cabinet near the sink. Which drawer? *Get a grip, Sadie!* Bottom one on the right.

She picked through the clutter in the drawer. She grabbed the hammer. The nails proved more difficult to get ahold of, especially after she knocked over the little box they were in. Her grandmother had kept them handy for hanging her collections. Framed photos, antique dishpans and most anything else that caught her eye. Sadie hadn't changed a thing except the placement of that one painting. It was her home now but the concept of change still felt wrong, disrespectful somehow.

Appalled all over again at her door now that she could see the full extent of the damage, she thrust the tools at Lyle. The feel of his fingers on her skin as he plucked the nails from her palm made her shiver in spite of the idea that they were in the middle of a crisis. Dummy!

"The way the door is damaged," he said, placing a nail and preparing to drive it into the wood, "this is the only way to secure it for now. It's not going to be pretty when I'm done."

"Do what you have to do." Suddenly deflated, Sadie regarded the chaos that had obviously blown through her kitchen. Someone had been in her house. The actuality sank in all the way for the first time. What could they possibly have wanted? She had no marketable values. No fancy electronics or jewelry. Heck, her television was older than she was. And if they had been looking for cash, this was the last place they should have come.

On the front porch, Gator and his crew were letting her know they didn't appreciate that she'd left them stuck in the barn. Rascals. It hadn't taken them long to figure out there were places in that old barn even Gator could wiggle through. "I have to let the dogs in."

This was crazy. She shook her head as she stamped through the house. If she found out Billy Sizemore or one of his blockheaded friends did this, she was seriously going to shoot at least one of them, maybe both.

The grandfather clock bonged quarter before the hour. Nearly three o'clock in the morning. Anger flamed higher, burning away the last of the fear and anxiety. Damn her daddy and his no-good friends. The notion that this might have something to do with why

Lyle was here elbowed her, since she apparently had tried to ignore that prospect. The jury was still out— way out—on that scenario.

With the dogs trailing her steps, she returned to the kitchen and the sound of her back door being disfigured. With his back to her, she didn't miss the butt of the weapon tucked into the waistband of his jeans. More fuel splashed on the anger already at a steady blaze inside her.

She waited out the final nail required to secure the door into its splintered frame. "So what happened?" Some parts were obvious, but there was plenty she didn't know. Such as what did he hear and see? Why didn't he warn her? And why hadn't he told her he had a gun? "How did my front door get unlocked? Did you see anyone?"

Lyle threaded his fingers through his hair, pushing it from his eyes. "How about I start with your last question first?" She didn't protest, so he went on. "I watched two males enter the house through the front door after some tinkering with the lock. It's an old lock, by the way. You need to take care of that."

Sadie motioned for him to go on and to shut up with the lectures.

"One man came right back out." He gestured ambiguously before walking over and up-righting the table and chairs. "The other was in the house maybe five minutes before I entered and tracked him down. In your room."

"My *bedroom?*" That was…nuts. There was nothing in her room worth the trouble of borrowing, much less stealing.

Lyle nodded. "We should make sure nothing's missing."

There wouldn't be anything missing. She had nothing anyone would want. She started to say as much, but she couldn't get past what she saw in his eyes. Fear. Worry. Uncertainty. Her breath trapped beneath her breastbone. "What is it you're not telling me, Lyle?"

"Sadie." He looked away. "Let's take this one step at a time. Right now—" those blue eyes zeroed in on hers with an urgency that unsettled her further "—we need to know what they were after."

The air jammed in her throat broke past its blockage and rushed into her lungs. "Okay. But then I want the truth."

Lyle checked the weapon at the small of his back as she led the way through the house. The living room had been ransacked. The first of the two bedrooms, as well. The bastard had just gotten to Sadie's room when Lyle interrupted him. She needed to confirm what he already knew. There wouldn't be anything missing in her room or the rest of the house.

The objective, he suspected, was secured in his truck.

Lyle had spooked the guy attempting to noiselessly break into his truck. He hadn't gone into the woods after him, considering the other man was in the house and the possibility of Sadie waking up and coming to the house was too great. The second had gotten a little trigger happy with his escape after bursting through Sadie's back door. Lyle hadn't fired his weapon. Instead, he'd caught up with and tackled the guy. He'd hoped to subdue him and get some answers. Unfortunately it hadn't worked out that way. It had come down to either shooting him or letting him go. The former was out of the question since the intruder was fleeing the scene. Lyle damned sure couldn't protect Sadie from behind bars. Gus would have the sheriff looking for a way to nail him.

Sadie was shaken. He saw her hands tremble more than once as she sorted through her belongings, putting things back in order as she went. Lyle helped as best he could and as much as she would allow. He didn't ask any questions, just let her do what had to be done. The skimpy lingerie she stuffed back into a drawer introduced another reaction into this already explosive mix. He worked at suppressing the response, but it wasn't as easy as he'd hoped.

When her home was set to rights, she shrugged. "Nothing's missing. Not that I can tell, anyway."

That wasn't the answer he'd wanted to hear, but it was the one he'd known was coming. He feared this break-in was about Sadie's past, not about her present.

She looked ready to drop, but she grabbed him by the arm and ushered him toward the bathroom. "Now we take care of your face."

He'd forgotten all about that. "My face will survive," he argued. The dead-last thing he needed was her touching him, particularly right now. As much as he'd like to profess complete objectivity, that would be a flat-out lie.

"You expect me to take orders from you—" she hesitated at the door and gave him a pointed look "—but I'm not allowed to give you any? Reciprocity, McCaleb. Look it up."

"Ha-ha."

"Sit." She pointed to the closed toilet seat.

Arguing would just be a waste of time. Her hard-headed determination had not mellowed with age. He sidled past her and did as she asked. "I could do this myself, you know."

She searched the cabinet under the sink. "No doubt. But then—" she straightened with a bottle of rubbing alcohol in hand "—I wouldn't get to do this." She dampened a washcloth with the alcohol and dabbed his cheek.

Though braced for the sting, he flinched, bit his tongue to hold back a hiss. "I'm glad you're enjoying this." Her hair hung around her shoulders, close enough he could have easily reached up and touched those silky strands. The slightest hint of the rose-scented soap she'd used, combined with the earthy essence of fresh hay, made his throat ache to tell her how good she smelled.

How much that sweet smell made him want to touch her. Another sharp sting from the alcohol caught him off guard, and he swore. Those plump, pink lips stretched into a smile. "Sorry," she said with absolutely no remorse.

"You really are enjoying this." He attempted to stay focused on the alcohol's burn rather than the one between his spread legs.

"More than you know." She made another nongentle swipe. "Just a scrape. You'll live."

"Thanks." He stood, but wished he had stayed put when the size of the room ensured his chest brushed her shoulder. Even that generic contact sent his heart into a frenzied gallop. He pretended to ignore the punch of high-charged electricity that jolted his body by surveying the damage to his face in the mirror.

She stared at him, or rather at his reflection. The hard questions were coming. He could feel her tension. He mentally scrambled for a way to evade the looming storm, but that wasn't happening, barring his suddenly dropping dead. On the other hand, since her shotgun sat in the corner by the door, that was not completely impossible.

"What is it you really want from me?"

If her voice hadn't sounded so small, so scared, so incredibly vulnerable, he might have gotten through this without meeting her eyes. The uncertainty he heard in her voice was confirmed right there in those jewel-green eyes, drawing even more deeply on his protective instincts. His fingers fisted in an effort to resist reaching out to her. He wanted to hold her. To promise her it would all be fine, but he couldn't make that promise. Her whole world was about to change, and there was nothing he could do to stop it.

"I just want to protect you." His throat tightened.

"What were those men after?" she demanded, sounding more like herself.

He wanted to blink. To break the spell, but that wasn't possible. "Like I told you, your father—"

"You're lying." She turned, brushing full against him, breast to chest, and stared up at him with a determination that would not easily be put off. "There's a lot more you're not telling me, and I want to know. Now."

"Sadie." He moistened his lips, to buy time and because he wanted to taste her so badly he could hardly endure the yearning. "You're right, there is a lot you don't know. I explained that I'm not at liberty to give you all the details at this time. I have my—"

"I don't care about your orders." She grabbed him by the shirt front and tried shaking him, maybe to make him see she wasn't taking no for an answer. All she succeeded in doing was sending him teetering closer to the edge. "Tell me the truth, Lyle. Tell me right now."

There was no time to develop an intelligent strategy to outmaneuver this precarious situation. No evasive explanation that would satisfy her. His only alternative was distraction.

His fingers dived into her hair. He pulled her mouth up to his and kissed her, hard at first out of sheer desperation, and then softer…because the taste of her melted him from the inside out. To his surprise, she didn't resist. She relaxed into him, the contours of her body molding to his but not where he needed her to be. His hands glided down her back, formed to her gorgeous bottom and lifted her against him. Right there. God help him, he wanted her. Right now. Right here.

She made a desperate sound that instantly hardened his already taut body. Her fingers threaded into his hair and pulled his mouth more firmly against hers. Desire and need swelled until he thought he might explode. He wanted to say things that hadn't been said seven years ago. Wanted to keep kissing her like this forever. Most of all, he wanted deep inside her…to have his body joined with hers the way he had craved before but couldn't.

She stopped and started to draw her mouth from his. His entire soul protested.

"Wait." Her voice was husky and breathless, her face flushed with the same desire raging out of control in him. "What're we doing?"

His diversionary tactic had worked a little too well.

"I shouldn't have…taken advantage of the situation." He knew this and yet he hadn't released her. He still held her tight against him in all the right places.

If she hadn't looked at him that way, he might have been able to resist kissing her again. He brushed his lips across hers. Her breath caught but she didn't draw away. Utilizing a restraint he wouldn't have thought he possessed at that moment, he kissed her tenderly. But there was nothing tender about the way his fingers kneaded her bottom. She arched against him and he almost lost his mind.

Then she froze, the change so abrupt his knees weakened.

Her gaze locked on his. "They didn't take anything from the house because that wasn't the reason they were here."

Her rationale ruptured the haze enveloping his ability to reason. Hellfire. She was right. "Dare Devil." The thought launched out of him, propelling him into action. He deposited Sadie on the floor and was out the narrow bathroom door before his next breath cleared the emotional bottleneck in his throat.

"I should've thought of that." She sprinted for the front door, almost getting ahead of him. "They lured us to the house to gain access to the horses."

He drew his weapon. "Stay behind me." His hand shook with the receding desire as he fumbled with the lock. He moved across the porch, then motioned for her to join him.

The barn doors stood open. Damn it! Sadie was right. Neighing resonated in the early-morning darkness. The sound of scrambling hooves warned more than one horse was loose.

Sadie called to the horses, at once calming and luring the animals with soft words. Lyle moved on to the barn and turned on the lights. The stalls stood open, every single one empty, including the last one.

"He's gone," Sadie said from the door, her face drawn with worry. "The others are all here, but Dare Devil is gone."

Fury bolted through Lyle. Damn Gus Gilmore.

Chapter Seven

Bucking Horse Ranch, 5:15 a.m.

Dawn was taking its sweet time arriving. Sadie didn't care if it was still dark. She wasn't waiting another second, much less a minute. She'd wanted to do this over an hour ago but she'd needed to get the other horses settled first and then Lyle had given her a hard time about calming down first. When he wouldn't turn over her truck keys, she started walking.

Before she'd gotten a hundred yards, he'd rolled up next to her in that fancy truck of his and ordered, "Get in."

She'd thought about telling him to go away and never come back, that she didn't need him or anyone else. But the truth was, as mad as she was, she understood she couldn't do this alone—not if she was smart. If she just hadn't allowed that kiss to happen. Maybe she could have fooled herself for a little longer that she didn't want him…but she'd showed her hand. And now he knew what a truly pathetic person she was.

Sadie closed her eyes and cleared her head. It wasn't the end of the world. She had been a fool before. Seven years ago she had pleaded with him to stay, to ignore her daddy's decree and her age. What an idiot she had been. The more important issue just now was getting that horse back. Dare Devil, like all her other rescues, deserved to live out the rest of his days in peace without performance expectations. She'd just gotten started with her rescue work really. The long-term goal was to make her ranch a haven for abused and neglected animals from all over Texas. Eventually she hoped to start a camp for underprivileged children where they could learn about the animals and the animals could enjoy their love and attention, a stark contrast from the strict life they had known in the rodeo. Sadie wasn't trying to be a martyr or to call attention to herself. With this ranch she'd inherited she had an opportunity to do something good. And maybe to make up for her father's lack of compassion.

The idea that part of her motive included doing exactly the opposite of what he wanted her to do, to take over his ranch one day, niggled at her. She dismissed the notion. This wasn't about him or her. It was about the horses.

From the moment Lyle turned onto the road at the end of her driveway, the land that stretched across the landscape on each side of the pavement belonged to the Gilmore family.

To Gus, actually. Since Sadie was the last in that line, so far and Lord knew she wouldn't be in her daddy's will, that left only him. She wasn't sure who that was the saddest for, him or her. At the moment she could not care less. Her mind was on Dare Devil's safety. If that horse had suffered at the hand of any of Gus's men, she would make him pay if it took the rest of her life.

Lyle slowed for the turn into enemy territory. Sadie stared out into the darkness. Her grip tightened on her trusty shotgun. The chances of her getting the horse back were next to none. Gus was too smart for that. But she had to try. Going about this the proper way required focus, despite the ungodly hour and the formidable man—she stole a glance at the driver—who would inevitably get in her way. The heat he'd generated when he'd pulled her against him swirled even now if she allowed the mental images to filter through her head. How could she still want him so very much? Maybe if she'd paid attention to her social life instead of ignoring those basic needs, she would have been better prepared for this. For him.

Focus, Sadie! This was definitely not the time to be distracted by neglected hormones.

Though it was fairly early, Gus would be up. Work started at the Bucking Horse by daybreak, around six-thirty. By that time the crew had better be dressed and fed, because there were no acceptable excuses for being late. *Late* equated to *fired.* That rarely happened, since the whole county knew the way Gus Gilmore operated. He stood by the motto that hard work never hurt anyone, idle hands were the devil's tools and all that holier-than-thou stuff. Sadie had nothing against hard work or anything holy, of course—though the only time she'd gone to church in her life was when her grandmother had taken her. What steamed Sadie the most was men like her father pretending to be something they weren't. He didn't keep a pew warm on Sunday mornings, but that didn't stop him from believing he would be the first through the pearly gates on Judgment Day.

The drive up to the mansion was a full mile. She didn't need the sun to know that every blade of grass in the pastures on each side of the paved minihighway sporting the Gilmore name would be the same height. The lush grazing pastures would be clean of horse droppings. The Gus Gilmore world had to be perfect. There was no room for the slightest flaw. Up ahead the house sprawled across the land a full eight thousand square feet, the exterior a pristine bride-white with massive columns and expansive porches. The barns and other outbuildings were a brilliant red without a single chip of missing color and not a lick of fading evident, since they were repainted every spring. No one, save visitors, was allowed to park a vehicle in front of the house, particularly one that might lessen the impact of elegance and sophistication. A little piece of the Hamptons in central Texas.

All the working pastures and corrals and stables, including the bunkhouse, were well beyond the main house. Like a general in charge of his troops, Gus conducted surprise inspections to ensure all met with his rigid standards. Lack of order and cleanliness were other reasons for a speedy departure from his employment. His expansive, powerful world operated his way and his way only. Failure to agree with him would cost a person his or her position, even the position of daughter.

Sadie fought the sting of tears. She would not cry. The rift between them was his doing, his decision. After her mother's death, he seemed to focus that impossible-to-please self-righteous conviction on her. Nothing she did or said had been right. Whoever said that blood was thicker than water had never met Gus Gilmore.

"Stay put," Lyle said, shutting off the engine, "until I determine how this is going down."

"Whatever you say."

Lyle stared at her for a moment as the interior light faded to black. She held her breath, hoping he would buy her no-questions cooperation. After a moment he reached for the door handle and got out. She restrained the urge to bail out immediately despite the new blast of fury detonating inside her. As soon as Lyle had started up the wide steps leading to the porch, she was out of there. She bounded around the hood just as the massive double doors leading into the house's grand entry hall opened. The ostentatious overhead porch light came on and Gus himself stepped out to stand beneath its spotlight.

Sadie took aim even as Lyle whirled toward her and ordered her to put down the shotgun.

"Where's Dare Devil?" she demanded of the man who cared more about power and position than his own daughter or any animal he'd ever owned.

By the time her furious words had stopped vibrating the air, Lyle was down the steps and at her side. Gus's cohorts had appeared from around both corners of the house, weapons readied for trouble.

"Put it down, Sadie," Lyle urged. "This is not the way to handle this."

"Not until I have an answer." She didn't look at Lyle. Her full attention remained fixed on the man standing on the porch, hands on hips as if surveying a pile of horse dung his help had overlooked.

Unafraid of what he likely perceived as a nuisance,

Gus descended the steps. He glanced to his left then his right, giving those gathered to protect him a slight nod. The men faded back into the darkness on each side of the house. Then he lowered his attention to Sadie. There wasn't a more arrogant man alive.

"What's the problem?" Gus walked right up to where they waited. "It's not even daylight yet. What is it you think I've done now?"

For a second Sadie couldn't speak. Why had everything changed between them all those years ago? When had he stopped loving her? Loving anything or anyone? Just because he'd lost his wife hadn't given him the right to quit loving his daughter. Sadie had lost her mother and she had still loved him...until he stamped the life out of those feelings. No one else around here had the guts to stand up to him. As dysfunctional as it sounded, she had made that another of her quests. She relished every opportunity to undermine his superiority and arrogance. Didn't he get it that she'd been trying to send him a message all these years?

She squashed those weaker emotions. "You stole Dare Devil. Where is he?" This, she had to admit, was low even for him. Wielding her shotgun and making threats appeared to have become the norm for her.

Gus shook his head. "You're the thief, little girl. Not me. You stole him from me."

If she hadn't known what a liar he could be, she would have sworn he was telling the truth. "You're avoiding the question," she charged. "Did two of your men trespass onto my property and steal him?"

"What do you mean trespass onto your property?" He swung his interest toward Lyle. "Is this your doing? You know mine and Sadie's relationship is on rocky ground." He took what he likely hoped to prove an intimidating step toward Lyle. "You'd like nothing better than to finish tearing us apart." He jammed a finger in Lyle's chest. "Is that why you're here? Who are you representing, McCaleb? Maybe your own selfish interests. I know for a fact you have an agenda, so don't deny it."

Lyle laughed, but there was no hint of amusement in the strained sound. "You don't need my help destroying your relationship with Sadie. You're doing an amazing job of that all on your own. And as for my agenda, Sadie knows why I'm here. What you do or don't know is of no interest to me."

"Maybe you've got Sadie fooled, but not me," Gus warned.

"This is not about Lyle or me," Sadie argued, not about to let this turn into a what-did-I-ever-do-to-you session. "Where is Dare Devil? I know you took him, so don't bother lying."

Gus turned back to her. Even in the faint light she could see the fury in his dark eyes. "Whatever our issues in the past, you're wrong about this one."

He was lying. There was no other explanation. "Then you won't have any problem allowing me to check the barns and other outbuildings. Maybe even the house." She added that last bit just to be a smart aleck.

He didn't answer, just glared at her with that same disappointment he'd showered upon her since she was twelve years old. When she was certain he would deny her request, he turned back to the house. "Billy!"

Sizemore swaggered from the shadows. "Yes, sir."

"Escort my daughter around the property. Whatever she wants to see."

With that stunning announcement, Gus walked back into the house and closed the door.

The impact of his decision shook Sadie far harder than it should have. He hadn't denied her request. What the heck? He never gave in that easily.

"Load up and follow me," Billy suggested, "unless you want to walk."

LYLE WASN'T SURE WHAT Sadie's intent was here. If Gus was responsible for the break-in and the horse's disappearance, there was no way he would bring Dare Devil here to his ranch. Lyle settled behind the wheel of his truck as she and her shotgun loaded into the passenger seat. He started the engine and executed a three-point turn so that he could catch up with Sizemore in his dually beyond the back of the house.

"Dare Devil isn't here."

He'd been about to say the same thing, though he hadn't expected it to come from her, considering she insisted on checking the property. "Yeah, I know."

Sadie watched out the window instead of looking at him. "But that doesn't mean he didn't do it."

Well now, he couldn't debate that conclusion. "So we go through the motions?"

"Yep." She twisted around in the seat and stared back at the house. "As convinced as I am, I'm not taking his word for anything." Sadie faced forward. "Gus would take that as a sign of weakness."

Lyle wondered if Gus's relationship with his daughter would have turned out differently if she were his own flesh and blood. Did he know the truth about her former identity? How had he and his wife been chosen to be a part of this? Had someone selected the Gilmores based on their financial status and approached them? What reason would Gus and his wife have had for going along with the offer? Sadie was the only child they'd had. Was there a reason for that? Was that reason the explanation for how they had come to be involved with a backdoor adoption? There were a lot of questions, and so far Lyle had no answers.

The one thing he knew for an absolute certainty was that he was in deep trouble with Sadie. What he'd irrationally intended as a distraction—however self-ishly motivated—had proved without question that he couldn't maintain his objectivity, much less his profes-sionalism, when it came to her. That made an already perilous situation *crazy* dangerous. If she decided to confront him about what happened, he would be in even more trouble. He'd already skirted the truth about why he was here. Outright lying about that kiss was out of the question. He suspected she wouldn't like his answer.

As REQUESTED, SIZEMORE escorted them to every build-ing and corral on the property. Dare Devil was not on the Gilmore ranch, unless he was tucked away on the proverbial rear forty. Lyle wasn't surprised. Gilmore was far too smart to have allowed himself to be caught so easily. Sadie had called off the tour after more than an hour of futility. It would take days to carry out a thorough search of a ranch the size of this one. The horse would be tucked some place out of reach until the dust had settled. Lyle got it that Sadie had needed to see, to show Gus she wasn't going to take this sitting down. The two had this business of one-upping each other down to a science.

"Stop at the house."

He sent her a questioning look and she added, "I have to talk to him."

Lyle parked in front of the house and prepared to get out, particularly if she opted to hang on to that shotgun.

"Alone."

A frustrated breath puffed out of him. "We've been over this already. I don't want you out of my sight."

"This will only take a minute and I'll be inside the house. He's my daddy, he's not going to kill me."

Lyle shook his head to stop the voice suggesting that her real daddy had been accused of exactly that. "Two minutes, and I'm coming in after you."

"Fine."

She climbed out of the truck and hustled up to the entry doors of her father's home. The house where she'd grown up. With parents who had kept a dark secret from her. Lyle scrubbed a hand over his face. How was he ever going to tell her the truth? He thought of the album hidden in the storage compartment behind his seat. Whatever happened, even if he told her right now, the result would be the same as if he'd told her the instant she came to her door yesterday morning.

There would be no forgiveness for the messenger. Particularly one who had shattered her life once already.

GUS SAT BEHIND THE BIG polished desk in his study, as he did every morning at this time, savoring coffee brewed from freshly ground beans imported from some place she couldn't pronounce and scanning the morning paper. Sadie burst in without a knock or announcing herself. "Wherever you took him," she warned, "you bring him back unharmed before dark today and I won't go to the sheriff and press charges."

Carefully placing his fragile and expensive china cup—from France, if she recalled—in its saucer, he let go of the newspaper and settled his attention on her. He studied her a moment over the tops of his reading glasses. "I don't have Dare Devil, Sadie. You should consider the other possibilities before making accusations. He may not be a competitor anymore, but his reputation carries some value." He removed his glasses and neatly folded them before placing them on the desk. "I'll make some inquiries and see what I can find."

The laughter burst out of her. She couldn't help herself. The man wanted to be a comedian now? What else would explain his sudden need to play daddy. "I don't need your help, Gus Gilmore. I need *my* horse back."

Another of those long assessing looks sent her frustration level skyrocketing. "You are in way over your head, little girl. Do you know who Lyle McCaleb is *now?*"

"Don't try to change the subject." He loved to play mind games. Well, she wasn't playing his games. Besides, he'd hated Lyle seven years ago, and she doubted that had changed. This diversionary tactic was nothing she hadn't expected. "This isn't about Lyle."

"Are you certain? What was his excuse for showing up after all this time? Don't you think it's ironic that he suddenly comes back after you've inherited your grandmother's property? That makes you quite a financially secure woman with valuable assets. Not to mention he knows how I would loathe you falling for him again. I don't want to see him hurt you."

This time she laughed for real at his comment. She was basically flat broke. A few folks donated feed and hay to her on a fairly regular basis for the horses. The tiny trust took care of property taxes and insurance along with a few other basic necessities. The only *asset* she owned was that ranch, and she wouldn't sell it for anything. She would always find a way to survive. Oh, and her grandfather's old truck, which was on its last legs, belonged to her. "Where is the horse? I'm not letting this go."

"As I said, I'll look into it." He sipped his coffee. "Meanwhile—" he set his cup aside once more "—why don't you ask your friend what interest the Colby Agency has in you? Or me, for that matter."

A frown furrowed its way across her brow. "What's the Colby Agency?" Lyle hadn't mentioned that name. He was here in an official capacity for some branch of law enforcement, but she wasn't giving Gus a speck of information.

Gus made a disparaging sound. "I knew he'd leave that part out, which, my dear, smacks of deceit." He shook his head. "I expected as much. He'll do nothing more than break your heart again, and, foolishly, you'll allow him to do just that."

Sadie held up both hands. She wasn't listening to this. "By dark today," she reminded him.

"Watch yourself, little girl." Gus stood, pinned her with an intensity that made her uneasy. "The Colby Agency is a private investigations agency. McCaleb's client is anonymous, so far as I can ascertain. I haven't been able to glean any information on that aspect of his assignment just yet. But there is a client and whoever that client is, your friend is being paid to be here and do whatever it is he's doing or planning."

Sadie didn't believe him. Lyle wouldn't have lied to her about that. What would have been the point? She couldn't tell Gus why he was here…she'd promised, sort of.

"I'll be waiting," she reminded him.

Before he could throw out some other bit of purposely twisted information, she left. She'd done what she came here to do. This nonsense about Lyle he'd tried to confuse her with would prove more of his lies. Even knowing how Gus loved proving she had no real friends, the mere idea that there could be some smidgen of truth to what he said made her sick to her stomach. Made her want to cry hard, but, by God, she would not.

She didn't utter a word as Lyle drove back to her house. The sooner she was out of this truck the better. She couldn't breathe. Couldn't think. Gus had planted the seed, and like that damned bean stalk story her mother had read to her as a kid, the seed had sprouted into something overwhelming.

Wrenching the door open before the truck came to a complete stop, she slid out, staggered a little and headed for the barn. Her stomach roiled with the bitter silt of remembered betrayal. Gus was a no-good, lying, mean son of a gun, but he never made that kind of mistake. She didn't want to admit it. With the fading of the initial shock, reality had taken root. If he said Lyle worked for a P.I. agency, it was likely true. It was always the murky details he warped into his own version of the truth. Something as cut and dried as place of employment was too easy to prove. Gus wouldn't waste his time.

Lyle had lied to her.

He'd kissed her as if he meant it—as if he still had feelings for her and wanted her. He'd been back in her life barely twenty-four hours, and he'd already lied to her.

Halfway to the barn, Sadie stalled. Set her hands on her hips and closed her eyes against the swaying landscape. Why had she let him fool her this way? Because she'd wanted to believe he'd finally come back for her. What an idiot she was!

"Sadie." Lyle moved in close. "What happened back there?"

She didn't want to open her eyes and see. His eyes, his face, the mere scent of him made her fuzzy-minded, made her want to fall into his arms and just forget. But that would be an even bigger mistake than the whopper she'd already made.

She forced her eyes open to the truth. The sun was up and showering its bright, unforgiving light over the land…over them. The worry she saw on Lyle's face was real, but that meant nothing. She'd been a fool for him, twice now.

"I want to see your official ID." Her chest ached beneath the ever-tightening band of emotions wrapping around and around her, keeping her unsteady. "Not your driver's license, but whatever proves who your employer is."

His hesitation told the tale before he uttered a single word. "What did Gus tell you?"

She turned away, couldn't bear to look at him.

"I want you off my property." She shot him a look that she hoped cut to the bone. "Now."

"I was sent here by the Colby Agency. A private investigations firm looking into exactly what I told you. I didn't lie to you, Sadie."

Renewed fury ignited. "No, you just left out the parts that didn't fit with what you wanted me to believe. You kept your mouth shut while I assumed precisely what you wanted me to presume. I filled in all the gaps you left." She slammed her hands into his chest, shoving him away from her. "You succeeded. Good for you." Too heavy to hold, she dropped her arms to her sides and dragged in a breath that hurt her heart. "Now get out of here."

"I can't do that."

The blast of outrage that burst inside her then made her tremble. "Don't you dare pretend you want to stay to protect me. I don't believe anything you say."

"It's the truth, Sadie." He reached out, tried to touch her. She backed away. "You're in danger. I can't leave until this is over."

And there it was. The other truth. He would leave when the job he was being paid for was done. The kiss hadn't meant a thing. His decision to take the job, if that part was even true, was about nothing more than the job.

When it was done, he would leave. And just like last time, he would take a part of her with him, leaving her damaged all over again. He'd been gone seven years, and it had taken a measly twenty-four hours for him to take her back to that same place he'd left her in all those years ago.

"I'm calling the sheriff. If I need protecting—" she

glared at him, barely kept her voice shy of a scream "—that's his job, not yours."

She walked to the house. Her pulse thundering in her ears, her body trembling with an agony that was all too familiar. He followed, not ready to give up. She doubted his employer would be pleased if he failed to get the job done. Well, that was tough. She wasn't about to do him any favors. One way or the other, he was out of here. Now. This morning.

She didn't need Lyle McCaleb.

Seven years ago she had been a wild, starry-eyed teenager who was so in love she couldn't see the forest for the trees. He had never loved her the way she loved him. He'd had other plans that didn't include her. She had been a distraction. A way to pass the time until better things came along.

She was a grown woman now. And she had other plans that didn't include him. If she died single and alone it would be better than risking his or any other man's betrayal ever again. To hell with them all!

"Sadie, be reasonable," he urged as she stormed up the steps to her porch. "This situation is too volatile and too dangerous to play games. That's Gus's style, not mine."

She turned on him in the middle of the porch, the dogs yapping as if there was no tomorrow inside the house. "Back off," she warned. Damn it, she'd left her shotgun in his truck. "We are finished. No games. No talking. No nothing."

That he looked away, beyond her, in the middle of her tirade only infuriated her all the more.

"What the hell are you staring at?" When he didn't

respond, Sadie turned around to see what was so fascinating behind her.

Mommy's coming for you, baby girl.

The words were scrawled across her front door. The red paint had dripped down the weathered white wood in an eerie manner straight off the screen of a horror flick.

"What the hell?" Sadie moved closer to the door, reached out and touched the paint. Still sticky. She smelled it. The air in her lungs evaporated.

Not paint...*blood.* The message was written in blood.

Chapter Eight

Victoria Colby-Camp reviewed the assessment report compiled by the research department. The investigation conducted by the detectives in charge of the Princess Killer case twenty-two years ago was as close to flawless as any she'd reviewed for that period, considering the science and technology they had to work with at the time. A joint task force from several counties surrounding the small community of Granger had come together to find the killer and eventually the bodies.

Over the course of ten years, more than a dozen young girls had gone missing. The M.O. was always the same—the girl simply vanished with not a single clue left behind. The victims were loosely connected by age, but even the ages weren't consistent. Social status was all over the place, some from very poor families, others from considerably wealthy ones. Race, religion, none of it was truly consistent. The killer's territory extended over several counties. In the end, the single thing all the victims had in common was that each one had a family dog adopted from a small veterinary clinic located outside Granger. But that connection had not been discovered until after the anonymous tip that led the police to the Barkers, the owners of that unpretentious clinic.

Raymond Barker was a beloved member of his community. His wife, Clare, was always at his side. Their small clinic barely stayed afloat, considering the extensive rescue work the couple performed. The family, including their three little girls, never failed to be present on the front pew at church. The children's clothes appeared homemade, their shoes hand-me-downs. Veterinarians from surrounding counties often suggested those looking for pets drop by and have a look at the many available at the Barker Clinic. Rafe and Clare's compassion for animals was known far and wide beyond the boundaries of their small hometown. Since the visits to the Barker Clinic and the disappearances were sometimes months, as much as a year, apart, the remote connection wasn't detected by the authorities.

The case might have gone unsolved if not for that anonymous tip provided early one morning. That tip brought the authorities to the old farmhouse owned by the Barkers. Photos of each "princess" as well as thank-you letters sent by the victims to show their appreciation for their new pets were discovered in the Barker home. The remains recovered from the property were identified as eight of those who had gone missing. The half dozen other missing girls from the surrounding area had not been recovered to this day.

Once the news broke, parents remembered their daughters interacting with Dr. Barker. He'd affectionately referred to their daughters as "princess," prompting investigators to call the case by that moniker. Each victim whose remains had been recovered from the property, as well as several whose remains were still missing, had written to thank Dr. Barker, weeks, sometimes months after the pet adoption. The letters were presumed to be the tipping point—the impetus that solidified the selection process for a heinous serial killer.

Victoria closed the file and her eyes. The images and words were gruesome. How could anyone, much less a mother or father, have committed such horrific acts? The evidence that connected Clare to the murders was far more circumstantial than that connecting her husband. Ultimately that was the reason she eventually won an appeal. There were those who would never believe her innocence, however, simply because of her dark past. Clare Barker's parents, the Sneads, had been murdered when she was barely thirteen. Some who knew the family always suspected that Clare had somehow been involved in their deaths. Given that the latter surfaced only after the arrests, Victoria had to wonder if that were the case at all.

Though a quiet, seemingly work-oriented family, the Barkers had earned the respect of their neighbors. Not social folks by any means, Rafe and Clare had stayed to themselves when not working, ostensibly completely focused on and devoted to their children. But the findings inside the home had told another story. Closets turned into prisons for the girls when they were in the way. Evidence of other, despicable abuse was also discovered. How had this travesty gone on for so many years without anyone noticing?

A rap on her door drew Victoria from the disturbing thoughts. She smiled as best she could as Simon Ruhl entered her temporary office. It would eventually be his conference room. For now he graciously lent it to her and Lucas whenever they were here.

"Is there news?" Victoria had spoken to Lucas earlier that morning. Had something happened since that call? She sincerely hoped not.

Simon settled into a chair across the table from her. "Research just uncovered a small but stunning piece of information. We may have a lead on Janet Tolliver's connection to the Barkers."

Victoria hoped this would prove the break they had been eager for. There had to be more information out there, and they needed to find it. Otherwise, their investigation was going to end similarly to that of the detectives more than two decades ago. "Finally." Tolliver's name was not mentioned in the previous investigation in any capacity. "Does this give us a starting place?"

"Actually," Simon said as he passed a report across the table, "it gives us another ending place. Janet Tolliver was Clare Barker's biological sister, older by two years."

How was that possible? "The police never found that connection? That's quite a strong tie to be overlooked."

"The Sneads were different," Simon explained. "They lived more or less outside society. Religious extremists. The girls were homeschooled. Clare was three and Janet five when they were separated. No one noticed. The Sneads, minus Janet, of course, moved to Austin. Nine-plus years later the parents were murdered. Clare was found covered in their blood and in a semicatatonic state. She spent several months in an institution before being introduced into the foster care system. Meanwhile, the Tolliver family took Janet in as their own. Eventually the adoption was legalized through a private attorney."

"Have you spoken to Lucas?" The need to hear his voice was suddenly a palpable force in Victoria's chest. "Have you briefed him on this new information?" Lucas was doing surveillance on Clare Barker. He needed to know immediately that there was reason to believe she was quite possibly dangerous, no matter that an appeals court had overturned her verdict and the evidence against her alleged past deeds was wholly circumstantial.

"I briefed him first," Simon assured her. "I felt he needed the information, pronto."

Of course he had. Victoria had worked with Simon for many years. He was well versed in the critical steps in a case such as this. She was unsettled this morning. The case file on the Barkers had gotten to her in a very personal way. The evil acts committed against children hit far too close to home, considering her own son had been missing for twenty years before finding his way home. During that time, Jim had suffered every manner of atrocity.

Victoria had to find and hang on to her objectivity. Funny, she and Lucas were supposed to be retired, and here they were embroiled completely in this case. But this one was different. Victoria sensed that there was a profound injustice here, and she needed to set it to rights. To do that, she needed clear, unbiased focus.

"How is Lyle doing with Sadie?" Victoria wanted these women protected above all else. Finding a way into their lives so quickly had not been an easy feat for the Colby Agency. Since Lyle had a history with Sadie, his way in had proven a bit more of a natural entry.

With the other two, the investigators had no choice but to watch from a distance until they were accepted, which made their protective efforts much more difficult.

"Lyle hasn't checked in this morning but all was under control last night."

"How is the confirmation process going?" Research was attempting to verify the thumbprint in each photo album provided by Janet Tolliver to that of the women allegedly the long-missing, presumed-dead children of the Barkers.

"Laney Seager's was easy," Simon explained. "She was arrested on assault charges as a teenager. Olivia Westfield's work mandated a background check, which required fingerprints. Sadie we can't confirm until Lyle gets fingerprints to us. She has seen her share of trouble with the law but her father has kept her from being arrested." Like everyone else working on this case, Simon looked tired. This kind of case was hard on the emotions. "I feel confident with the other two having been confirmed, that it's a safe bet to assume Sadie will be a match, as well."

The story was an incredible one. The sheer number of confusing layers was nearly overwhelming. Victoria could now better understand how so much was overlooked twenty-two years ago. The connections were vague, disjointed and deeply buried.

The reality of the investigation at this point was that investigators were in place with all three women. Clare Barker was under surveillance. And Rafe sat in prison, another day closer to death.

Still, if Clare didn't kill Janet Tolliver and with Rafe in prison, one of the two had contacts who willingly committed murder. Janet Tolliver had been expecting a visit from the Colby Agency, which seemed to indicate Rafe was the one to order her murder. Clare had no way of knowing Victoria had met with Rafe. But why have her murdered and at the same time have her expecting help from the Colby Agency? Not reasonable or logical. But then, what about this case was?

With Clare's chilling past, it was an easy leap to conclude that she was the most likely of the two. But then the justice system had deemed her not guilty, if not entirely innocent. Rafe was the one whose guilt no one questioned. Then there was the letter. Victoria could not get past the letter when considering his guilt or innocence. That gnawing instinct went against how the evidence had stacked up against him. Victoria's instincts were never that far off the mark. Had Clare purposely been setting up her husband to take the fall if she were ever caught? Could either of them been so blind as to not know what the other was up to, considering the evidence of abuse taking place inside the home?

"We still have no connection between any of the adopting parents and Janet Tolliver. All three of the Barker children were legally adopted in private transactions. The paper trail was difficult to follow, but having the birth certificates provided by Tolliver is helping. Olivia, the oldest, is the only one who knows she was adopted. She has never sought her birth parents."

Victoria rubbed the back of her neck. That would change soon enough. Would that be when the next tragedy in this ongoing travesty occurred?

No matter how hard the Colby Agency tried, there

was no protecting these women from the reality of who they were when true justice finally found its place in this complicated and chilling story.

Allison Ingram, Simon's secretary, appeared at the door. "Simon, Lyle McCaleb is holding on line one."

Simon thanked her. He and Victoria exchanged a worried look.

What now?

Chapter Nine

Second Chance Ranch, 8:50 a.m.

Lyle had tried to reason with Sadie for more than an hour. She refused to listen. He sat on the porch now, her final order still resounding in his ears.

Leave! And don't ever come back.

He'd just gotten approval from Simon to do what he'd hoped to put off until the danger had passed.

Lyle pushed to his feet and walked to his truck. His hands shook as he unlocked the storage compartment behind the driver's seat. He removed the leather pouch containing the album. How had he come to be the person who would exert this shocking blow? Chance? Fate? Whatever the reason, he prayed that God would give him the wisdom to do this right and the strength and opportunity to protect Sadie afterward.

He hesitated at the door, took a deep breath, then rapped on the wood still marred by the threat the sheriff had taken one look at and chalked up to one of Sadie's many enemies pulling a prank on her. Sheriff Cox had additionally suggested that the missing horse was the same. He'd show up, Cox had declared.

Clearly the man had concluded exactly what Gus

Gilmore had told him to conclude. Gus had been using his power to manipulate Sadie for years. To his credit, he had protected her once or twice when she'd pursued her goals a little too passionately. But manipulation was manipulation. Neither Gus nor the sheriff understood that some of the events occurring now were about far more than Gus and Sadie's relationship. The danger was real.

Had Gus learned that the Colby Agency was looking into Rafe Barker's request? Discovering that Lyle worked for the Colby Agency had probably been easy. But to learn the case he was on and to use some aspect of it to scare Sadie, that was just plain evil. As stern and hard as Gus Gilmore had always seemed to Lyle, this was a new low even for him—if he was the one responsible.

Sadie opened the door and glared at him, fury emanating from her whole body. At least now she wasn't toting her shotgun. "What is it going to take to get you out of my life, Lyle McCaleb?"

"You wanted the truth." He indicated the package he held, emotion crowding into his chest. "I've been authorized to give you that now, if you're sure that's what you want." Misery dumped another load on his shoulders.

She stared at the leather pouch he held, the color seeping from her face even though she had no idea what was inside. Deep in her heart she suspected something was off with her history. Lyle had sensed that uneasiness since his arrival early yesterday. Her frustration with life in general was about a little more than Gus or him.

"You have five minutes," she said as she stepped

back and pulled the door open wider, "to convince me to hear you out. Don't test my patience."

"Fair enough."

"If I think for one second that you're giving me the runaround, I'm done," she added, leading the way to the living room. "So don't waste my time." She plopped down on the same old sofa he'd waited on seven years ago when he'd dared to visit her at her grandmother's house. Adele Gilmore had liked him, he'd learned. He wished she were here now to referee. And maybe to explain some of the missing details. Sadie was going to need someone to lean on through this. He hoped she would allow it to be him.

Lyle had considered at length the best way to start when it came to this part. None of the options were ideal, but starting at the beginning seemed best. During his call to Simon earlier this morning, he'd learned yet another piece of the puzzle. Janet Tolliver and Clare Barker were related by blood. The layers were slowly peeling away.

He sat down on the opposite end of the sofa. "Twenty-two years ago," he began, "a man and his wife, Raymond and Clare Barker, were arrested for multiple murders." He removed the copies of the newspaper clippings from the leather pouch but left the album inside for now. He spread the clippings on the coffee table. "You might want to look over these."

Sadie picked up the first article. "This is the woman you mentioned might have some bone to pick with Gus?"

Lyle steadied his breathing. "Yes."

The black-and-white photos in the articles wouldn't show Clare Barker's green eyes. Sadie had those green eyes. And the blond hair. When they got to the photo album, she would see. His fingers clenched on the case. He'd give most anything not to have to show it to her. But there was no way around it. Part of him wanted to be the one to help her through this, but the more selfish part hated to be the one since she would most assuredly despise the bearer of this news long after the dust had settled.

After reading through the articles, Sadie looked up and asked, "They still haven't found the other bodies?"

He shook his head. "A lot of folks had hoped that Rafe would eventually suffer some sense of remorse and give up that information. But he has never acknowledged or denied any of the murders. Clare has claimed innocence the whole time. She stood by her word that she had no knowledge of the murders."

Sadie stared at the decades-old black-and-white photo of the infamous couple. "How could they do this? What kind of monsters are these people?"

The agony churning inside him twisted more deeply. "I can't answer that question, Sadie."

"How could no one have suspected what they were doing?" Her head moved side to side. "Those poor little girls. There's no telling what they endured before they were murdered."

Lyle understood that she was referring to all the victims, and the Barker daughters in particular. He held his breath and waited for her next question.

"I can't see how Gus would be connected to these people." Her gaze leveled on Lyle. "What is it that you're keeping from me?" She searched his eyes. "I knew there was something. You're not a very good liar."

He opted to take that as a compliment. "A few days ago my agency received a letter from Rafe Barker." Lyle closed out his emotions. He couldn't do this otherwise. He explained the contents of the letter, summing it up with, "He swears his daughters are alive and that he fears Clare intends them harm."

Sadie frowned, her confusion visible. "How does that connect her to Gus? He..." The bewilderment cleared and disbelief took its place. "You're looking for the daughters."

Lyle nodded, unable to speak.

"You think..." The article she'd looked at last slipped from her grasp and floated to the floor. "That's impossible. I have baby pictures. They're all over the place at Gus's house. Me and my mother. Me and Gus. The three of us." Anger lit in her eyes. "You've known me my whole life. You know this is not just a mistake. It's crazy."

Lyle braced his hands on his knees and held on. He wanted to hold her and make her understand how sorry he was to have to do this. "Barker gave us a name. Janet Tolliver."

Sadie shook her head adamantly. "I don't know anyone by that name."

"I know," he said gently. "She was murdered the day before I arrived here. But she left something to help us find the truth." He withdrew the album and offered it to her. "This is the connection."

Hands trembling, Sadie took the album and settled it on her lap. She stared at the first page that displayed Sarah Barker's birth certificate. She turned to the next page. She gasped, one hand going to her chest.

Lyle couldn't suppress the crash of emotions. The

best he could hope to do was conceal the outward display of the turmoil whipping inside him. His best effort wouldn't chase away the burn in his eyes.

Sadie's life would never be the same.

THE LITTLE GIRL IN the photos could be her twin. Some part of Sadie knew that wasn't the case. Hot tears spilled down her cheeks and perched on her trembling lips. How could this be? She moved from page to page, photo to photo. Someone had taken pictures of her all through the years. Who had been close enough to take such intimate family shots?

Sadie swiped her face with both hands, then closed the album. She took a breath for courage and turned to the man waiting quietly on the other end of the sofa. "You should have told me this the moment I opened the door and found you on my porch." With each word, the rage built deep in her soul. How could he, of all people, hide this from her for one minute, much less a day?

"The risk to you was too great," he offered softly. "I couldn't take the chance that you would refuse to cooperate given how you might react to this information."

He spoke so damned softly she wanted to slap him. There was nothing soft about any of this! "What risk? I still don't get that part." The whole story was insane. Her mother and father were Gus and Arlene Gilmore. This was a mistake!

"Rafe Barker is convinced his wife intends to do what he allowed the police to believe he had done twenty-two years ago just to have her final revenge against him. He thinks she knew from the beginning that he could not have murdered his daughters. His theory is that she realized he tipped off the authorities all those years ago, and he claims he did, and that she has worked relentlessly to get free just to settle that score."

No way this involved Sadie. None of this sounded or felt familiar. "It's a terrible tragedy, no question. But the names, these photos, they don't stir any memories." She tried to show Lyle with her eyes what he might not get from her words. "Don't you think I would feel something if there was any truth to this cracked story?"

"You were just two years old, Sadie. You might not remember anything even when prompted by evidence like this." He gestured to the album. "I'm not an expert on matters like this. The one thing I know with complete certainty is that you'll need help with this. Counselors." He shrugged. "I don't know. But we have to get through this threat to your safety first, then there are tests you can have that will confirm what I'm saying to you."

Sadie tossed the album aside as if it were poison and might absorb into her skin. "You mean threats like the message some nimrod left in blood on my door?" Cox insisted the words weren't written in blood, but Sadie knew better. He'd promised to have it analyzed, but she didn't need a test to prove what she recognized any more than she needed a test to establish that she was Gus Gilmore's daughter. Whether it came from roadkill or a human, the message was written in blood. Lyle agreed with her, not that she had needed his endorsement, either.

"The message on the door tells me she's found you. And somehow she's keeping an eye on you despite being under surveillance by the best the Colby Agency has to offer. Obviously she has someone working for her, in view of the fact she hasn't left her apartment since we started surveillance."

"I want to talk to her. Right now." Sadie fought back the fear her own words ignited. Her body shook from it. "I want her to say that nonsense to my face."

Lyle held up both hands. "No way. We can only speculate that she left that message. If it's unrelated, we don't want to hand her your identity or your location."

Sadie got up. The talking was over. It was time to take action. "Who else would know to leave a message like that?" That option wasn't even plausible. Other than Lyle and his employer, who would have access to this pack of lies?

Lyle stood, looked her dead in the eye and said, "Gus."

That was the one prospect she hadn't considered, and it took the wind right out of her sails. "That doesn't make sense. Why would he do that? He definitely knows I'm his daughter."

"He's bound to have some idea why I'm here. He tossed out the Colby Agency name as you recall. He's a powerful man. He may have decided to use the situation to his advantage in this war you two have going on."

The idea that her own daddy would have sent one of his hoodlums to do this fired her up all over again for completely different reasons. She had to calm down and think rationally. What if this crazy tale was real? She pushed away the idea. "On the other hand, if he wants to take this place away from me, I guess he could just say that I'm not really his daughter—if any of this is so, which it absolutely is not."

"He legally adopted you. That makes you his daughter in the eyes of the law."

Wait, wait, wait. "How do you know that?" How in the blazes did he know all this stuff about her and she didn't? Because it wasn't real. She refused to believe that her entire life was one huge lie.

"It was done legally, but carefully hidden through private channels."

"And you found it?"

"My agency did." He plowed his fingers through his hair. "As far as the law is concerned, you're as much a Gilmore as Gus. If—" Lyle emphasized the *if* "—he's behind any part of this, it's because he wants to provoke the kind of reaction that would give him what he needs to overturn your grandmother's will."

"What kind of reaction?"

"You threatening to shoot anyone who crosses you. If you were considered unstable, any of the judges he knows would gladly appoint him a conservatorship."

Sadie shook her head. As often as she'd wanted to kill him, she would never really *kill* him. He was her father, for what that was worth. She would never do him physical harm. And she'd never shot anyone else. Half the time that old shotgun of hers wasn't even loaded. That uneasy feeling nudged her a little harder when she considered how many of Gus's friends considered her a little wild and crazy.

"I'm not unstable." She just had a bad temper when it came to protecting the animals.

"You'd end up in the institution of his choosing and he'd take over this place." A frown marred Lyle's face. "Do you have reason to believe he wants your grandmother's will overturned badly enough to go to extreme measures?"

Sadie had to think about that one. That she'd stood on his property with her shotgun aimed at him filled her head. If he was trying to make it look as if she'd gone over the edge, Lyle was right. That incident probably hadn't helped her reputation. "He's made the statement on several occasions that my grandmother had no right to do this. This land was supposed to go to him first."

The whole concept made her furious. As angry as she was, that didn't come close to blotting out the pain of the other. She didn't want to feel it. She didn't want to know it. "I need to talk to him." If there was any truth to this, he would confess if confronted with evidence. Or she'd hold him at gunpoint until he did. No, Lyle was right. That would be a mistake. If Gus wanted her out of the way that badly, she had to watch her step.

Would he really go that far?

She struggled to clear her mind. "Gus can straighten this out." Lifting her chin in defiance of the emotions warring inside her, she decided on a course of action. "I'll bet he can explain all of this. He'll make you see that this is a mistake." Gus would explain everything. Lyle would see.

Lyle moved closer, placed his hand on her arm as if to comfort her. She drew back. Couldn't bear to feel him. She wanted it to be because she was angry and felt betrayed by him all over again. That wasn't exactly what she felt. The truth was she didn't trust herself. If she let him touch her, she might just collapse into his strong arms. It would be so easy, but she couldn't do that. Strength and determination were needed here.

Her whole life was on the line and she had to figure out how to deal with this…this movie-of-the-week drama. Sensory overload was already an issue. Did she scream? Cry? Run away?

Calm down. She had to calm down. And think.

"If Gus doesn't know why I'm here," Lyle explained in that low, quiet tone that made her want to shake him, "he doesn't need to know. There are already too many complications cropping up. Any additional trouble could create a chain reaction. We don't need Gus's money and power delving into this right now. And we damned sure don't want the media getting involved. We have to keep this low profile for you and for the others."

The others. Sadie hadn't considered the others. The Barkers had three children. This had to be a mistake.

Pounding at the front door shattered her efforts to pull it together and concentrate. Before her brain had strung together a reasonable reaction, her feet were taking her toward the sound. Maybe the sheriff had come back with those test results? Not likely. He'd left only about half an hour ago. Damn, she'd lost all perception of time and certainly all grasp on reason.

Before she could open the door Lyle cut in front of her, opened the door with one hand while resting the other on the butt of the weapon tucked into his waistband.

Gus Gilmore loomed in the doorway. "What the hell is going on over here? I got a call from Sheriff Cox. Said I'd better get over here and see this for myself."

Sadie slipped around Lyle before he could step in her path. "Why don't you tell me?" Lyle cut her a look, and his words of warning about the others echoed in her mind. Oh, God. How did she do this?

Gus stared at the door and shook his head. "How on God's green earth would I know?" He nodded toward Lyle. "Why don't you ask him? All the trouble started after he got here."

He had a point with that statement. Confusion zoomed around in her head, making her hesitate. Things around here had been a little weirder than usual since Lyle showed up at her door. But he had nothing to do with Dare Devil or her grandmother's will or this awful story that couldn't possibly be right. What would he have to gain? Had he told her who the agency's client was? Gus had made a big deal out of that. Wait, yes. Rafe Barker. Her stomach roiled at even the thought of the man.

Sadie wanted to cry. To fall to her knees and beg her daddy to fix this nightmare. To make Lyle believe her. But there were other lives at stake. She stiffened her spine and grabbed on to her composure with both hands. "This is between you and me, old man." Her voice still sounded a little shaky. Not nearly as shaky as her emotions just now. She glared beyond Gus to the two henchmen who had accompanied him. "Did you do this, Billy Sizemore?"

He sniggered. "Damn, girl, I spent the best part of the morning escorting you around. How the hell could I have done anything over here?"

Sadie blinked, refused to be flustered by the lug-headed bully, even if he was right. That didn't mean one of his pals hadn't done it for him. "What about you?" she demanded of the man at his side, Chip Radley. "Where were you this morning?"

"Taking care of business for me," Gus answered for him.

Her attention shifted back to her father. He was livid. She knew that face. Her throat felt dry and tight. Gus Gilmore wasn't her father, if Lyle had his story right. The pictures and the newspaper article swam before her eyes. Some awful killer was her daddy. She shuddered, hugged herself to hold her body still. "What kind of business?" She had a right to know, seeing as Gus Gilmore was the prime suspect, in her mind, where this whole mess, Dare Devil and all, was concerned. By God, she had a right to know his business under the circumstances, even if he didn't understand that fact.

"As soon as you told me what happened with Dare Devil, I sent Radley out to check on some folks low-down enough to do such a thing."

It took every lick of self-control Sadie could rummage up not to demand what he'd learned. But that would be the same as admitting she didn't really believe he was the one responsible. Maybe he wasn't. What did she know? She didn't even know who she was. "You mean, besides you?"

A glimmer of emotion, so faint she wondered if she had imagined it, flickered in his eyes. "I have a few leads to follow up on." He turned away from her and said to his men, "Clean up this mess before anyone else sees it." He muttered something about sacrilege.

"No." Sadie's announcement had him turning back to her. "I'll clean it up myself. I don't need anything from you."

Gus held her gaze for an eternity, something sad and disappointed in his. That was nothing new. He'd been disappointed in her for most of her life. Maybe now she had a clue as to why.

She didn't move until they had driven away. Her knees went weak, making her sway.

"Whoa." Lyle caught her and pulled her against him. "I think maybe you need to take it easy for a bit. I'll clean this up."

Weakness, she hated it! Sadie pulled away from him, squared her shoulders. She was not weak. Whatever happened, she could handle it. "I'm perfectly fine."

"Neither of us has had much sleep," he argued gently. "Let me do this for you, Sadie."

"Just go away, Lyle." She set her hands on her hips and exhaled the breath she hadn't realized she was holding until now. "I need to do this. If I'm still, I'll just obsess on that photo album."

He backed off. "I understand. I'll take care of the horses and feed the mutts."

Damn. She had lost all track of time. Swallowing her pride, she said the right thing for once. "Thank you."

She watched him as he walked to the barn. The way he moved had always made her burn for him. There was a sleek fluidity to the way he walked. His strength had made her feel safe and cared for. Something her father had turned off when she'd needed him most. Mercy, she couldn't hang on to a thread of thought. Her mind was all over the place.

Sadie dragged her weary body back to the living room and collapsed on the sofa. She stared at the photos on the pages of the open album. Her as an infant. The man and woman with her and the other two little girls were strangers to her. Maybe the baby wasn't even her. Sadie closed her eyes. Yes, it was her. There were several photos of her as a baby in the Gilmore family album. Just none with Gus and Arlene until she was two or so. Now she knew the reason why.

She felt like a stranger in the living room—parlor, as her grandmother had called it—that she'd loved as a kid. All the trinkets. Little statues and framed photos, the graceful old oil paintings. It all seemed suddenly foreign to her. Had her grandmother known about this? Of course, she had. You don't come home with a two-year-old and announce you've just had a baby.

The ache swelled so big and so fast inside her that Sadie couldn't breathe. How could this be? All that she had thought she'd known...all that she'd trusted was a lie.

Sadie propped her elbows on her knees, put her face in her hands and did something she hadn't done since Lyle left her all those years ago.

She cried.

THE HORSES WERE HAPPY to see him. Lyle managed a smile. He'd missed being around the animals. He shook his head. Somehow, he had to manage a visit with his folks. He'd let far too much time pass already. Work was always his excuse. But with what was happening to Sadie, he suddenly felt the need to hug his mother and even his father. A handshake just wouldn't be enough.

It took all his willpower not to go back to the house and hug her. She'd fight him like a wildcat, but he knew that was what she needed. The stubborn woman just refused to admit it. He took his time feeding the

horses. Gave them all a quick rubdown and their free-
dom into the pasture. He folded the blankets they'd
left in the stalls and hung them over the railing. Sadie
kept the place so clean there was little to do in the way
of mucking out the stalls, but he did it more or less to
put off going back to the house too soon. Maybe she
needed some time alone to think. He couldn't blame
her. He'd sure needed a minute when he'd first heard
this incredible story.

Gus showing up had given Sadie an excuse not to
do anything rash. For once, Lyle was thankful for the
old bastard. As much as Sadie wanted to believe her
daddy didn't love her, Lyle was pretty damned sure he
did. He just had a hell of a way of showing it. He was
immensely grateful that she hadn't demanded answers
about the photo album from Gus. He wasn't sure his
warning about the danger had gotten through the emotions bombarding her, but it seemed he had.

Looking at the whole situation between Sadie and
Gus from Gus's prospective, Lyle supposed he had
withdrawn emotionally after his wife's death to protect himself. It wasn't the right thing to do, but folks
didn't always do the right thing. Maybe Gus was only
guilty of taking this competition between him and his
daughter too far. But then, who had taken Dare Devil?
The horse was worth a few bucks, even as old and worn
out as he was. Could have been any outlaw out to make
a fast dollar.

Lyle would enjoy learning it was Sizemore. Kicking
his butt would feel good. But that would be too easy.
Nothing about this situation had been easy so far, and
he suspected that wasn't going to change.

He'd like nothing better than to wake up in the

morning and find that this was over for Sadie. Every minute that she suffered tore him apart a little more.

The dogs hadn't done any yapping, which he had decided to use as an alarm while he was at the barn and Sadie was in the house, but he didn't like having her out of his sight.

Rain clouds were moving in. This time of year it wasn't unusual for a storm to blow up. Since the barn roof was in good shape now, there were no worries about leaks. Maybe he could talk Sadie into taking a ride to town for lunch. Her cupboards were bare as hell.

Before climbing the porch steps, he checked his boots. His mother had drilled that habit into his head as a kid. *Don't bring anything in this house that belongs in the barn or the pasture, young man.* This was a strange time to think of something so mundane. Maybe mundane was what both he and Sadie needed.

She had scrubbed the blood, and he knew it was blood, from the door, but the fresh coat of paint was still in the can sitting on the porch. Sadie wasn't in the living room or the kitchen. His pulse hitched instantly, but his gut told him she was here. That was something he remembered from before. He could feel her presence. Whenever she was close, his pulse reacted. That the connection was still there after so many years was just further proof of what a fool he had been to walk away. He should never have allowed Gus to exert such influence over his decisions.

On the way to her bedroom he found all three dogs waiting outside the bathroom. Water spraying sounded on the other side of the door. Guess she'd decided she couldn't stand any trace of that mess on her skin. He could use a shower himself.

He tapped the door. "Hey, save me some hot water!"

"Maybe," she shouted back.

Despite having sensed she was okay, relief rushed through his blood at hearing her voice.

"Come on, boys." He glanced at the Chihuahua. "And girl."

Finding the dog food wasn't easy. By the time he did he understood why Sadie kept it hidden above the fridge. Gator, the Lab, was as adept at opening the lower cupboard doors as Lyle.

He poured the kibbles into the different-size dog bowls.

The mutts chowed down. Lyle wasn't a fan of kibbles, but he had to confess to a hunger pain or two. To tide him over he guzzled down a glass of milk. Good thing he was consuming it. The expiration date was only a day away.

Sadie showed up just in time to catch him going for a second glass. She was dressed, hair back in that loose ponytail, jeans snug on her slender body and a plain white tee that looking anything but plain on her. He finished off the milk and put his glass in the sink.

"You hungry?" he asked, knowing she had to be.

For a long time she stood there, watching the dogs, as if she hadn't heard him. Then she lifted her gaze to his. "I want to go to Granger."

"Granger?" That little hitch he'd experienced in his pulse a few minutes ago hit him again, only harder.

"I want to see the house."

That was what he figured. "Sadie."

"Don't try talking me out of it. You're either going with me or I'm going alone."

"There's nothing there to see," he countered. "It's been over twenty years."

"One of the newspaper articles said the house was bought by the parents of some of the victims. They boarded it up, didn't want anyone else to ever live there, but they didn't want to burn it down." She moistened her lips. "They wanted folks to remember what happened in that house."

He moved toward her, had to. He needed to touch her. His fingers curled around her shoulders and squeezed with all the reassurance he could convey in that small gesture. To his surprise she didn't resist. "Sadie, I know this is tearing you apart inside, but you've already had to absorb a lot today. I don't think this is a good idea."

"I'm going."

There was no use fighting it. He couldn't deny her, whatever she asked. "If there's no changing your mind..."

She searched his eyes, hers bright with desperation. "I need to remember something...anything. I have to try."

Chapter Ten

Granger, Texas, 2:00 p.m.

"It's smaller than I expected." Sadie craned her neck
to see all she could beyond the truck's broad windows.
Lyle had just driven past the welcome sign for Granger
proper. *Where history lives.* That cold sensation Sadie
had been fighting all day crept through her veins now,
making her feel chilled, no matter that the sun shone
strong and bright. The town's population hovered just
under two thousand. Really small. Too small to have
been the home of a monster like Rafe Barker.

"You drive through here before?"

"I don't think so. Maybe." If she'd been here as an
adult, it had definitely been a drive through and she
hadn't been the one driving. Nothing looked familiar.

The queasiness that had started the instant she read
the message painted in blood on her door was still her
companion, but Lyle had been right about eating. She'd
forced down a burger and it had helped.

She glanced at the album lying on the console between them. A couple of times on the drive here she'd
started to pick it up, but each time she'd lost the nerve.

"Drive slower." She didn't want to miss anything.

The town was an old one with a few historic features still intact. She'd noticed the railroad tracks before. Lyle had explained that this had been an important cotton-trade intersection back in the day when the railroad ruled mass transit.

Another of those icy shivers went through her as they passed the police department. She wondered if any of the policemen who'd been involved in the arrest twenty-two years ago were still on the force. Did any of the teachers at the schools remember the older girls? Probably not, she decided, since none had been old enough to go to school.

A church caught her eye and she pondered whether or not it was the one the Barkers had attended. Had she sat on one of those pews as a toddler? She squeezed her eyes shut. No, no, no. She had gone to church with her grandmother.

Eventually the little town gave way to open road. She turned to Lyle. "How much farther now?"

"According to the GPS—" he tapped the dash "—about two miles."

Sadie's heart kicked into a gallop. Oddly, her mind kept tripping over the irony that the Barkers had rescued dogs, cats and other small pets. The concept made her throat hurt. Was that kind of thing in one's DNA? *Breathe, Sadie. Don't think about that part right now.*

Lyle flipped on his right-turn signal and slowed. A big old farmhouse sat off the road, flanked on all sides by ancient trees that shaded the aging tin roof and the overgrown yard. The wood siding might have once been white, but it was more gray now and peeling badly. The windows and front door had been boarded up, just as the article she'd read had said.

Lyle parked in front of the house. The driveway had disappeared in the thick grass. Beyond the house she could see the roof of a barn, not red like hers at home, more a brown. According to the newspapers, the veterinary office had been operated out of a renovated barn. The property was fenced for horses, but there had been no mention of horses in any of the articles.

"You want to get out?"

She'd been certain about the answer to that before they left the Cove. For some reason she wasn't so sure now.

"We don't have to."

"Yes." She gathered her courage. "I need to see."

Lyle opened his door first. He got out and came around to her side. Despite her determination, she hadn't moved. When her door opened, she managed a stiff smile. "Thank you." He didn't say anything, but the worry in his eyes said all she needed to know. He was here for her. Whatever happened, he had her back.

There was still a sparse layer of gravel beneath all that overgrown grass. It crushed under her boots. The sky was clear but the air seemed thick and sticky in her lungs, no matter that the temperature was relatively mild for late May and there was a robust breeze. The front porch leaned to one side, so it wasn't surprising that the floorboards creaked as she walked toward the boarded-up door.

Overhead, remnants of birds' nests and spiderwebs hung on every available ledge and in every nook between old, cupped boards. The front of the house beneath the porch had been whitewashed recently to cover up vandalism, but the ghost of graffiti lingered just below its surface. Sadie thought of the bizarre message left on her door, and that frigid rush ran through her again.

She wandered to the end of the porch and stepped back down to the overgrown grass. The house was deeper than it had looked from the road. Back home her barn stood a good distance from the house. Here the barn-turned-clinic was only fifty or so feet from the house. A screened-in back porch overlooked the yard, where more massive trees offered shade from the Texas sun. Between the house and the barn the hand-stacked rock skirt of a well interrupted the flow of knee-deep grass. A bucket, bent and abused, hung from a frayed rope. The well drew her in that direction. She rested her hands on the cold stones and looked into the seemingly endless black hole.

Had they looked for bodies down there?

A squeak hauled her attention to the far side of the yard. A child's rusty swing set stood beneath a tree, the broken slide squeaking with each puff of the wind. Her boots grew heavier as she walked in that direction.

For a long time she stood there. Just looking. Then she touched one of the swings, set it into motion. Laughter whispered through her mind. Her heart jolted at the imagined sound. Had to be her imagination. Or had she hung on in one of these swings while her older sibling pushed her forward and laughed as she squealed with equal measures of fear and delight?

Dragging a shaky breath into her lungs, she turned to Lyle, who stood by patiently while she explored. "Can we go inside?"

Lyle cocked his head and considered the boarded-up back door beyond the wall of ragged screening. "We can try. It's called breaking and entering if we succeed. Malicious damage of property if we fail."

He smiled at her, and a burst of heat chased away some of the chill. "That's only *if* we get caught."

"I can't argue with that." He hitched a thumb toward the house. "I'll move the truck back here so we don't attract any attention and see what kind of tools I have."

As crazy as the idea was, considering where she was standing, she still enjoyed watching him walk away. The continuity of that feeling was reassuring. The breeze picked up. She hugged herself. The leaves rustled as the tree branches swayed. That whisper of child-like laughter swirled with the swishing of the leaves, making her shiver. A limb scraped the house, attracting her attention there. That window, though she couldn't see it for the rustic boards nailed over it, seemed kind of familiar. The limb scraping against the house felt incredibly familiar. There were no trees that close to her house or Gus's.

"Got a hammer."

Sadie gasped as the sound of his voice snapped her back to the here and now. He'd parked his truck near the swing set, gotten out and closed the door without her being aware he'd moved. She'd been completely immersed in a *memory* that shouldn't be hers. A glance back at the window confirmed that unnerving feeling.

"I want to go up there." She pointed to the window on the second floor that was barely visible between the leaves.

He held her gaze a moment, then offered the flashlight he had in his other hand. "Okay then."

The screen door whined as they entered the screened-in porch. At the door, Lyle dug the claw of the hammer beneath the first board and tugged. The board groaned then popped loose. Sadie flinched. Five more just like that—she jumped each time—and the door was exposed.

Sadie grasped the handle, anticipation detonating in her veins, and gave it a turn.

And it was locked.

"Give me a minute." He hung the hammer in his belt and body-slammed the door, twice.

The door burst inward and the musty smell of disuse wafted out to greet them. Sadie couldn't move for a moment. If she went inside, would she feel any different than she did now? Would she remember something that would confirm she was Sarah Barker and take away her sense of self?

Only one way to find out. Sadie stepped across the threshold. It was dark. She remembered the flashlight and clicked it on. The beam spilled across a cookstove. The kitchen. Made sense. Cobwebs clung to the bead-board ceiling and walls. A thick layer of dust covered everything else, including the floor. She rubbed at the dust with the toe of her boot, revealing the green-and-yellow pattern of worn linoleum beneath. Images flickered, disturbing her vision. She blinked repeatedly, shook her head.

"You okay?"

"Yes." Sadie elbowed aside the heebie-jeebies and focused on the room. Typical farm-style kitchen. Stained and chipped porcelain sink. Old laminate countertop with metal trim. Ancient fridge, reminded her of her grandmother's. Big wooden table with chairs on each end and benches along the two sides.

"Looks like the place was left as it was that morning."

Sadie nodded. "Seems so."

"Why don't I lead?"

"Sure." Sadie thrust the flashlight at him. She didn't need it anyway. None of this was familiar to her. No. She shook her head. She'd probably seen the linoleum somewhere. Maybe at the home of one of her grandmother's friends.

The kitchen led into a long narrow hall that divided the house down the middle and ended at the front door. Or began there, depending upon the way you looked at it. Along one side of the hall a staircase climbed to the second floor. Doorways on each side of the hall near the front door led to twin parlors. One was furnished more formally with what Sadie generally referred to as old-people furniture. Uncomfortable and out of date. The other was obviously the one the family had used most often. Sagging sofa. Box television set. A recliner. Bookshelf lined with the expected, mostly books about dogs and cats.

The house was spooky quiet. She hugged herself and wrestled with the trembling that had started deep in her bones. She started back to the hall before Lyle. He caught up with her in time to prevent her from tripping over a broken floorboard.

"Watch yourself," he warned.

Her attention drifted upward.

"Upstairs?" he asked, directing the flashlight's beam that way.

Sadie nodded then remembered that unless he shined the flashlight at her he wouldn't see the gesture. "Yes." She cleared her throat. "I want to see the other rooms."

Lyle checked each tread before moving upward. Ensuring the steps were still stable enough to support their weight. Sadie couldn't get a deep enough breath. The dust, probably. Couldn't be anything else.

At the top of the stairs was the first bathroom they'd encountered. A rubber duck sat amid the dust and rust in the tub. Three doors lined the corridor. The first appeared to be the parents' room. Plain. Faded wallpaper coming loose in one corner where a water leak had stained the wall.

Sadie backed away from the door. She didn't need to go in there. She followed Lyle to the next door. A bed and chest of drawers were the only furnishings. A guest room, she supposed. There was no window. Lyle checked the closet, closed the door before she had a look.

"What's in there?"

"Junk mostly."

Something she'd read in one of the articles bobbed to the surface of the turmoil in her head. She reached for the door and opened it. With obvious reluctance he pointed the light into the small space.

Ropes and chains lay on the floor. Articles of clothing were twisted into gaglike devices. Her heart bumped hard against her sternum. This was where the children had been imprisoned. Clare Barker had denied the charge, but the evidence had proved otherwise. She wondered why the devices were still here. Hadn't they been used in court as evidence? Or had they used photos instead?

She closed the door and walked out of the room.

"You okay?"

She ignored his question. But no, she wasn't okay. Saying it out loud wouldn't help. "That's the one." Sadie moved toward the final door. The window of this room would look into the massive branches of the tree next to the house.

The room was the same size as the parents' room. There was only one bed, full size. A chest of drawers was the only other piece of furniture, just like in the windowless room. At some point the walls in this one had been painted pink. The toe of her boot bumped something on the floor. She leaned down and picked up the stuffed dog. Her hand shook so hard she held it more tightly than necessary to hide the tremors. More toys were scattered over the floor. She turned to the bed, the covers tousled.

I'm 'fraid. The words whispered through her mind. Images of baby-doll pajamas and long blond braids flashed like images cast on the wall by an antique projector. Screaming. Not children's screams. A woman's. *Let me out! Let me out!*

Sadie reached for Lyle's arm. Her fingers curled into his shirtsleeve. "I'd like to go now."

She couldn't get out of the house fast enough. She needed air and there was none in this place. It was a tomb. Misery and death lingered with the dust and cobwebs.

Sadie rushed out the back door and through the screen door, letting it flap closed. She gasped for air and struggled to restrain the heaving that threatened to humiliate her. She braced against the big tree trunk, the one closest to the house, while Lyle banged on the boards until they covered the door sufficiently.

Beyond the barn, deep in the woods would be the burial ground where the remains of those eight young girls were found.

Sadie stared up at the window of the children's room.

That had been her room. She blinked, understood that cold hard truth with utter certainty. This had been her home.

With at least one murderer.

9:30 p.m.

SHE WAS FINALLY ASLEEP. Lyle covered Sadie with a blanket. The old sofa couldn't be that comfortable, but he didn't want to risk rousing her by carrying her to her bedroom. The day had taken a lot out of her.

Gus had called twice. She had refused to talk to him. Lyle kept expecting him to show up at the door, but that hadn't happened. When they returned from Granger, she had pored over the newspaper articles. She'd asked him dozens of questions he couldn't answer.

Then she'd finally given up the battle with exhaustion and wilted on the sofa. He was damned tired, too, but that demand would have to wait. The dogs had been fed but the horses needed tending and the barn secured for the night.

When he was sure she was down for the count, he grabbed her house key, locked the doors and headed for the barn. What had to be done would take only a few minutes. Make sure the animals had food and water, close the doors and then he might try catching a few minutes of shut-eye in the upholstered rocker that had been Adele's favorite chair. She'd crocheted the doily draped over the back of it. He remembered Sadie complaining that she'd attempted to teach her to no avail.

Sadie wasn't the domestic type. She preferred rubbing down horses and mucking stalls to crocheting and serving tea. All the Gilmore women had been genteel Southern ladies. But not Sadie. She had been too full of life and curiosity to sit still long enough to play refined. She loved getting her hands dirty and her body sweaty.

Lyle had fallen in love with her the first time he laid eyes on her at the Long Branch Saloon. He'd just turned twenty-one and had bought his first legal beer. Sadie and a couple of her friends had gotten in with fake IDs and claimed a table next to the dance floor. One dance was all it had taken, and every cell in his body had burned to tame the girl. But she was having none of that. No one was going to tame Sadie Gilmore.

They had met for several dates before he found out her real name and the truth about her age. Fifteen. Beautiful and dangerous to a guy over the age of legal consent. He'd tried to break it off with her, but she was as stubborn as she was beautiful. She'd teased and taunted him, and he hadn't been able to say no to anything she wanted, much less to their secret rendezvouse. The last night they had been together she had begged him to make love to her.

As much as he had wanted to, he'd refused. She was too young. Her daddy was already on to him. He'd threatened Lyle on more than one occasion. Not that Lyle could blame him. His daughter was barely more than a child. In his brain, Lyle had understood that. But his heart wouldn't deny her. He had known that final night that if he didn't leave he would cross the line. He couldn't do that to her or to himself. She deserved the chance to grow up and become the woman she was destined to be without him charting a different path for her. Gus had warned him that he would disown Sadie if she ran away with Lyle.

So he'd walked away and never looked back. It had been the right thing to do in his mind at the time.

But he'd never stopped wanting her...never stopped loving her. On her eighteenth birthday he had tried to call, but she'd been in Cancún or some party place. He'd left a message, even sent a card, but she never responded.

That was the last time he'd tried. He closed the barn doors and started back to the house. For some reason he hadn't bothered to get involved with anyone else. The occasional date here and there. A few one-night stands. Work kept him busy most days, and dreams of Sadie had filled his nights.

Sadie's old truck snagged his attention. The front fender on the driver's side was dented. He was pretty sure he would have noticed that if the damage had been there before. Running his hand over the bent metal, he leaned down to get a closer look.

The force of the blow to the back of his head rammed his forehead against the fender. He tried to raise up, turn around and defend himself, but the night closed in on him.

He had to get to Sadie. That thought followed him into the blackness.

"STOP." SADIE COULD hear the dogs yapping like mad but she was too tired to wake up. She needed to sleep. If she woke up she would have to remember.

She didn't want to remember.

Her chest burned. She coughed.

Abigail was sitting on her chest licking Sadie's face.

"Stop." She turned her face into the pillow but the dogs just wouldn't shut up. Abigail was dancing around on her chest. She wouldn't stop.

As if each one weighed ten pounds, Sadie forced her eyelids to open. She blinked. How long had she been asleep?

Not long enough apparently. She didn't want to wake up. Gator stuck his face in hers. Barked in that deep Lab roar.

"Damn it, Gator." Sadie sat up, ushered Abigail aside. She closed her eyes to stop the spinning in her head. What was wrong with her?

She drew in a deep breath to rouse her brain. She choked, coughed like the old man with COPD who shoed her horses. She swiped the tears from her eyes and blinked.

What the hell? Why was the room foggy?

She tested her next breath. More coughing.

Smoke.

Sadie shot to her feet. Staggered. The dogs went crazy.

She turned around in the room. Smoke came from every direction.

The house was on fire.

She tried to feel her way to the entry hall and kept bumping into furniture. She couldn't breathe. Couldn't see.

What was that adage she learned in school? *Stop, drop and roll.*

The dogs were tangling in her feet. Wait, she couldn't stop! She had to find a way out of here.

The front window. Sadie dropped onto all fours. The smoke was thinner down here. She scrambled to the window overlooking the porch. Keeping her head as low as possible, she reached up and pushed at the lower window sash with all her strength. Slowly, an inch at a time, it raised. She lifted the latch for the old-fashioned screen and pushed it out of the window's frame.

"Abigail, come." Sadie poked her upper body through the window, the little dog in hand, and deposited her onto the porch. Frisco was next. He jumped out of her arms and right through the window opening.

Gator was going to take some doing. "Come on, boy." She grabbed him by the collar and dragged his seventy pounds to the window. She patted the window ledge. "Jump, boy, jump." The smoke burned her throat, her nose and eyes. She couldn't get a breath. She needed this dog to cooperate.

Nothing was ever that easy with Gator. Once she got him to poke his head and front legs out the window, she basically lifted and pushed the rest of him out.

Sadie collapsed on the floor, wheezing and coughing.

She had to get up. Her brain knew this but her body would not respond to the commands.

"Get up, Sadie," she muttered.

Didn't work. Just made her cough some more. She was so tired. Her eyes were burning. Something crashed in the kitchen. There were strange crackling noises. Or maybe scratching...

She was in that yard behind the old Barker house. The wind was blowing and the tree limb was scratching the window. Her sister was pushing her in the swing. Only it wasn't old and rusty. It was shiny and new. Their daddy had bought it for Christmas. Another little blond-haired girl chased a dog around in the grass.

Her sister. Sadie had two sisters. Not Sadie. *Sarah.* Her name was Sarah.

Wait… Now they were in that old bed together. Someone was coming. She could hear the footfalls in the hall outside their room.

I'm 'fraid.

Hands were touching her, pulling and tugging. Sadie fought the hands. She didn't want to go. She was afraid. She told herself to scream, but her lips wouldn't form the sound.

Her head hit something. Her eyes were burning. She couldn't see. She fell. Hit the floor.

This was bad. She was going to die…again.

"Sadie!" The voice shook her mind awake. "Sadie, breathe!"

She gasped. Coughed so hard she vomited.

The hands rolled her onto her side. She wasn't on the floor anymore. She was in the grass. Where was the swing set? Where were her sisters? Why couldn't she open her eyes?

"Come on, Sadie. Talk to me!"

Bright lights blinded her. Colors flashed and the sound piercing the air hurt her ears.

Where was she? Home? Where was home?

The dogs were yapping again.

Something covered her face. The air smelled better now. She blinked at the sting in her eyes.

Why was she on the ground?

Who were all these people?

Fire.

Ice filled her veins. She tried to sit up. Strong hands held her down.

Sadie yanked the mask off her face and screamed, "Lyle!"

Dear God, he was still in the house!

"Calm down, Miss Gilmore," the man urged. "You're going to be all right."

Paramedic. She recognized the uniform now. Why wouldn't her brain work properly? People were everywhere. They were spraying the flames shooting up from the roof of her house with their big hoses. Others were shouting instructions. The dogs cowered close to her, but something was still wrong.

What was she supposed to remember?

Lyle. Where was Lyle?

Sadie scrambled away from the paramedic as he reached to put the mask back on her face.

"Lyle!"

She staggered to her feet, turned around and around, tried to spot his face in the crowd.

Where was he?

"Ma'am, please," the paramedic urged, "you need the oxygen. And you need to sit down."

She smacked at his hands. "I have to find Lyle. He was in the house, too." Why wouldn't anyone listen to her? Tears burned her cheeks. What had happened? She didn't understand this. Where was he? "I can't find him."

"It's all right, ma'am," the paramedic said, "your friend is safe. He's in the ambulance already. Got himself a bleeder, but he's going to be just fine. We had a time talking him into leaving you long enough to get stitched up."

Sadie tore away from the paramedic and ran for the ambulance. She stumbled, picked herself up and started running again. Gator, Frisco and Abigail chased her, yapping wildly. The paramedic shouted at her but she ignored him and everyone else tramping around on her property.

Lyle sat on the gurney inside the ambulance. A paramedic taped a bandage to the back of his head.

"Lyle." She felt weak. She needed to lie down.

He pushed the paramedic's hand away and turned to her. Sadie wasn't sure which one did what, but somehow she was suddenly in his arms and that was all that mattered.

"You scared the hell out of me, kid," he murmured against her hair.

"I'm not a kid anymore, I told you." She buried her face in his chest to hide the sobs she couldn't contain.

"Ain't that the truth," he whispered.

It definitely was, and the first chance she got she intended to show him just how much woman she was.

Chapter Eleven

Lucas Camp leaned forward, pressing his right eye to the telescope zoomed in on Clare Barker's first-floor apartment window across the courtyard. He'd leased the apartment directly across from hers, on the ground floor as well. She'd retired for the evening more than an hour ago. The lights had gone out and he'd watched as she closed the blinds.

He wasn't concerned about her escaping without his knowledge, since there was no back door with any of these apartments. Most were studios, a few one-bedrooms. There was a front entrance and one window. The building was brick. Any escape through the wall would require tools Clare Barker had not carried into the apartment with her and which would generate sound.

On his routine strolls of the grounds, Lucas surveyed the back side of the row of apartments that included hers twice each day. So far she hadn't come outside even once. No cell phone transmissions, no conversation at all. The parabolic ear focused on her apartment had picked up nothing at all. He had, how-

ever, picked up more than a few eyebrow-raising con-
versations from one or more of her nearby neighbors.
Occasionally, he got a glimpse of her at the window.

Her attorney had dropped by once. Otherwise there
had been no visitors. Lucas was not convinced by her
pretense of fading into the background like this. She
was up to something. He just hadn't latched on to a
decent theory yet. She was far too smart not to have a
plan of some sort. Whether it was the one her husband
alleged was yet to be seen.

Clare had graduated from Texas A&M's College of
Veterinary Medicine just like her husband. They'd met
in the program and married right after graduation. It
still rattled him that a man and woman who appeared
to have such compassion for animals could be such
cold-blooded killers. His instincts leaned toward the
idea that one of them wasn't. The only question was
which one.

Lucas settled into the chair he had positioned for the
view of his subject's apartment. He'd called Victoria
to wish her a good-night. She had sounded tired and
frustrated. The case had gotten under her skin far too
deeply.

A few hours' sleep and he would check in with her
again. Perhaps after some sleep Victoria would feel
more like herself. Before giving in to the need for
downtime, Lucas checked his equipment one last time.
If Clare Barker spoke to anyone, he would know it. If
she opened her front door, the motion sensor he had
placed on her door frame would trigger an alarm right
here in his place. She wasn't going anywhere without
his knowledge.

May 23, 12:23 a.m.

THE WAIL OF SIRENS startled Lucas from sleep. He sat up. Lights flashed in the courtyard. The sirens heralded the arrival of fire trucks and emergency responder vehicles. He checked Clare's door via the telescope. Still closed and her lights were out. He shut off the parabolic ear and grabbed his handgun. At the door he shoved the gun into his waistband beneath his jacket before stepping outside.

Shouting from the two-story building at the rear of the complex drew his attention that way. Flames were already leaping from the rooftop. Occupants had spilled into the courtyard. Rescue personnel and some occupants were rushing from door-to-door to ensure no one was left behind in the apartments.

Lucas watched for the lights to come on in Clare's apartment. He strode quickly across the courtyard, tuning out the panicked voices all around him. Being pent up in that apartment for the past sixty or so hours had made his gait stiffer than usual.

A *whoosh* loud enough to drown out all else drew his attention to the end of the one-story row of studio apartments on Clare's side of the courtyard. Most of the occupants on that side had already filtered onto the sidewalk in front of their apartments. Dazed and confused residents wandered all around the courtyard. Lucas hurried to cut through the gathering crowd, his attention focused on one door in particular.

"Sir!"

Lucas turned to the police officer who had shouted at him.

"We've shut down traffic. We need to get everyone

across the street. If you could help rather than moving toward the danger, it would be much appreciated."

Lucas thanked him and then headed toward Clare's apartment in defiance of his request. He would like to help, but right now he had to get to that apartment. Two more officers were already moving door-to-door from the end of the one-story row nearest the eruption of flames, checking the apartments to confirm they were empty.

One of the officers reached Barker's door at the same time as Lucas. "There's a female inside," he explained. "Late fifties. Clare Barker. I didn't see her come out."

"Step aside, sir."

Lucas stood aside while the officer banged on the door and shouted instructions for anyone inside. The two-story building a few yards away was already fully consumed. The fire was burning swiftly through the old one-story portion on this side of the courtyard.

"Let's go in," the second officer to arrive at the door ordered. On closer inspection, Lucas realized this one was a member of the rescue squad.

The handheld battering ram knocked the door off its hinges with one blow. The two official personnel rushed inside, one hitting the lights. Lucas was right behind them.

"The place is clear," the officer in the lead yelled.

The second turned and came face-to-face with Lucas. "Sir, we need you to move across the street. This is a dangerous situation."

"I just need a look," Lucas pressed. "She's a little off in the head," he improvised. "She could be hiding in the closet."

The men exchanged a look. The rescue responder said, "All right, but make it quick." To his colleague he added, "Watch him. Get him out of here as soon as he's had a look."

Lucas rushed to the bedroom area that was divided from the living room area by a built-in bookshelf. The closet was empty. No clothes, nothing.

He moved into the bathroom, ignoring the cop's threats to drag him out if he didn't come with him. The cramped bathroom was empty, the shower door pushed inward, revealing dingy tile and no Clare Barker. Lucas started to turn away, but he decided to pull the shower door outward and check that side of the shower stall first.

The tile had been removed in a small area. He dropped into a crouch and checked the hole. It went all the way through to the next apartment. Just large enough for a small, slim woman to slither through.

Lucas shook his head. He had watched the occupant of this apartment come and go. A much younger woman than Clare Barker, the woman who was identified by the apartment manager as Toni Westen had dark hair and carried at least fifty pounds more than the older woman. Lucas had been had.

The officer grabbed him by the arm and pulled him to his feet. "I will remove you by force, sir."

"Sorry." Lucas adjusted his jacket. "You were right, she's not here."

The cop shook his head and ushered Lucas toward the front door. The lights started to flicker. Three feet from the door Lucas stalled.

"Go," the cop shouted with a nudge at Lucas's back.

Lucas stared at the wall between the window and the door. Clare Barker had left a message.

On the wall four stick figures had been drawn. A woman and three little girls, stair-step in size. A big red X had been drawn across the stick figures.

Clare Barker was gone. Her destination and intent as clear as the drawing on the wall. A mother-and-daughters reunion.

CLARE SCANNED THE MOB gathered in the convenience store parking lot across from the burning apartments. She didn't see the man who had been watching her. He would never find her in this crowd or dressed as she was. She had slipped out twice already, just to test her disguise.

A hand clasped her elbow. She jumped and turned to face what she hoped would not be an officer of the law. It was *him*. Thank God.

He leaned close. "This way. We need to hurry."

With his hand clasped around her arm, he hurried her through the frightened people. They rushed around to the rear of the convenience store.

The lot behind the store connected to another that sprawled out in front of a strip mall. She removed her dark wig and the padding that gave the appearance of bulk and tossed them into one of the trash cans that lined the back of the store. She glanced up, thanked her Maker and hurried after her friend.

At the end farthest away from the fray at the convenience store, a small white car waited in the shadows. He moved quickly to the driver's side while she climbed into the passenger seat.

She couldn't draw in a deep breath until he had

driven around behind the deserted strip mall and eased out onto the street running along the back side.

Clare closed her eyes and started to pray an offering of her gratitude for her successful escape. She had waited so long… These past few days had felt like a lifetime.

"Will the police be looking for you?"

His voice drew her to the present and the steps that needed to be taken as swiftly as possible. "Not right away." She smiled at the driver, who had been immensely kind to her. "With all that's happened, I've failed to thank you properly."

He glanced at her. "We do what we have to."

Yes, that was true. "Do you have all that I require?"

"Everything on the list."

That was very good. "I will repay you one day."

He looked at her again as he braked for a traffic light. "I've already been well compensated."

It wasn't until then that she allowed her gaze to rest on his right shoulder. He was preoccupied with driving so he wouldn't notice. She had no desire to make him feel uncomfortable or to injure his feelings in any way.

Her visual examination slid down his right arm, which ended only six or so inches below the shoulder. He'd lost that arm twenty-three years ago as a young man. No one had ever known the truth about that day. Only Clare and him, and the person responsible, of course.

He and Clare both had suffered greatly. Those responsible would all pay. She would see to it.

Her time was finally here.

She relaxed into the seat as he drove her through the

night. The drive would take a while. Sleep pulled at her but she refused its tug. There was too much to do to waste time sleeping. As much as she fully trusted this man, it was best to remain alert and attentive.

Nothing or no one would be allowed to stop her.

"CLARE."

Her eyes drifted open to complete darkness. She jerked forward, but the seat belt confined her. "Where are we?"

"It's all right. You're safe now." He got out of the car. The interior light blinded her until her eyes adjusted. Her door opened. "Come on, Clare. It's okay. We're here."

She released her seat belt and slowly emerged from the car. He closed the door and took her by the hand with his left. "Hurry."

She followed alongside him, her feet getting tangled in the tall grass. When they had moved beyond the trees, the moonlight spotlighted their destination. Her heart shuddered to a near stop before bursting into a frantic race.

"You're home, Clare. You're really home."

She fell to her knees, tears streaming down her cheeks.

Yes. She was home.

Vengeance is mine, the Lord said.

But He had come to her in a dream and whispered in her ear. Because of the special circumstances, He had decided that vengeance would be hers this time.

And it began now.

Chapter Twelve

Second Chance Ranch, 10:00 a.m.

"I don't want to argue." Sadie turned away from him, stalled on the walkway that led to what had once been her front porch.

Lyle's head throbbed, and he hadn't managed any sleep for the past two nights. He wasn't at his best by any means. They'd spent eight hours at the hospital. Both had been checked out thoroughly. He had a mild contusion and six stitches where some bastard had whopped him in the head with a blunt instrument that had not as of yet been found.

Sadie suffered from a good dose of smoke inhalation. He closed his eyes and shook his head, winced at the pain the move prompted. If he'd been hit any harder and lost consciousness rather than just being rattled, she would be dead now. She'd gotten the dogs out, but the smoke had gotten to her and she hadn't been able to get herself out.

That was Sadie. Looking out for the animals before taking care of herself.

Her house was a total loss. A cleanup crew would arrive in a couple of days to go through the rubble in an attempt to salvage any personal belongings. Sadie had wanted to do that herself, but Lyle had talked her out of it. That was a job for professionals.

He moved up behind her, wanted to hold her more than he'd ever wanted to do anything in his whole life. "You want answers. I get that. But your sisters don't know what you know."

She whipped around, went nose to nose with him. His body tightened near the point of pain. "They should know. This is not a game. They have the right to know."

He worked at calming the emotions tangling inside him, but every minute with her was a struggle. The ability to maintain even a semblance of objectivity had vanished when he'd pulled her through that window. At this point, talking was not what he wanted to do. The atmosphere between them had changed, and there was no turning back. "Two of my colleagues are working 24/7 right now to get close enough to protect them. We can't screw this up. Their safety is at stake. If we get in the way...the worst could happen."

Those green eyes darkened and widened with her own mounting frustration. "Why aren't the police protecting them? If they knew the truth—" she waved her hand as if the remedy should be crystal clear "—they could agree to protective custody!"

Calm, Lyle. Stay on the point. "What do we tell the police? That a man on death row wants his three daughters—who the world believes were murdered twenty-two years ago—protected from their recently released mother!"

The hurt that shimmered in her eyes instantly doused his flare of irrational anger. She looked away. Lyle dropped his head back and blew out a blast of frustration. He had to get a handle on these damned emotions. In an effort to do just that, he pulled in a deep, hopefully calming breath. The air smelled of smoke and charred wood, and yet the sky was clear and blue, as if nothing bad had happened.

"Are they safe?" Her voice sounded too small, trembled. She lifted her gaze to his. "Can the people from your agency protect them right now? This minute?"

"Yes. These men are the best at what they do. They're prepared to risk their lives without blinking." Before she could launch a counter, he went on. "Clare Barker is at this moment unaccounted for. Whoever is working with her is, as well. If she knows your identity, we could inadvertently lead her to the others by making contact. We can't take that risk, Sadie. It's too great to them and too great to you."

She surrendered. The defeat showed in her slumped shoulders and the weary sigh that hissed past those pink lips. "She's just gone? This woman, Clare?"

Lyle nodded. He had briefed Sadie on the news from Lucas. "Simon, my boss, and Lucas reviewed the video security footage at the convenience store across the street from the apartment complex. She left with a man in a white or gray car. We didn't get a model or license plate number. The only identifying factors we did get were that her accomplice was tall, had light brown hair and that he was missing his right arm. He never looked back, so we didn't get a face or profile shot." Clare, on the other hand, had looked back, almost as if she knew there was a camera and she wanted whoever was watching to know it was her under that disguise.

"You think this one-armed man left that message on my door? Gus said Sheriff Cox got word from the lab that it was deer blood. God knows, there's always one getting hit on the highway. Finding a carcass wouldn't be that difficult."

Lyle turned his palms up. "We don't know who left the message. The one-armed man is certainly a prime suspect." There hadn't been any rain in days. The storm that had threatened earlier had blown around Copperas Cove. The ground was too dry for a vehicle to leave tire impressions. There was no way to say who or how many uninvited had driven up to Sadie's house. The sheriff and the fire marshal couldn't tell them anything conclusive just yet about the fire. One thing was definite, it was one hell of a coincidence that Sadie's house had burned within hours of Clare Barker's apartment complex going up in flames. Fortunately, no lives had been lost in either event. That in itself was an outright miracle.

Sadie gave her head a little shake. "I don't want to believe it was Gus. But the list of those who know about my birth parents is seriously limited. That message was meant to scare me, and whoever left it knew the trick to use."

Lyle recognized she was scared, even if she would admit it only in a roundabout way. He also grasped that even though she and Gus didn't get along, he was her father and she loved him. She just didn't like to say it out loud. "There is also the possibility," Lyle suggested, "that Barker is orchestrating certain things from prison. And don't forget the stick-people drawing Clare left on the wall of her apartment. We can't be sure of anything right now."

"Jesus." She chewed her bottom lip.

He bit back a groan. This wasn't the time to be feeling this way, but there was no stopping the intense response to the way she was torturing that lush lip. He was in no shape to be that strong. They were both exhausted and in need of clean clothes, which only made him think about stripping hers off. They'd had showers at the hospital, but their clothes reeked of smoke. Pretty soon they would need to find clothes and a place to stay.

"Have you seen him?" She searched Lyle's eyes, the question surprising him. "Do you think he killed all those girls?"

Somehow he had to find his focus, for her. "I watched the interview Victoria Colby-Camp, the head of the Colby Agency, conducted with him." Lyle lifted one shoulder in a shrug. "He was thinner than in the photos you saw. Older, of course. Hair was gray." He met that searching gaze. "He looked tired and resigned to his fate. But when he spoke of his desperation to have his daughters protected…there was a glimmer of the kind of compassion that you'd expect from a man who rescued small animals."

Her lips trembled and her face pinched with the misery his words had elicited. God almighty. He didn't know how to choose the right words to give her what she wanted and still protect her feelings. Would it have been better if he'd said Barker looked like the monster the newspapers reported him to be?

"And her?"

"Older, thinner. Gray." The prison photos he had seen of Clare Barker showed a woman who was every bit as determined as her youngest daughter—unfortunately, for the wrong reasons it seemed. He opted to leave that part out of his answer.

"Do you think she did it?" Again, she watched his face and eyes closely, looking for signs that he was keeping anything from her. "Could she have been the one doing the killing instead of him, like he said?"

Lyle implored her with his eyes to see the truth in what he was about to say. "I honestly don't know. But those girls didn't kill themselves. One of them, or both, has to be a killer."

She pressed her fingers to her lips to hide their trembling. Tears, glittering like tiny diamonds, perched on her lashes.

Damn it. He'd said too much again. "Sadie, you know who you are. As difficult as this crazy story is to reconcile, it doesn't change the person you are."

"Maybe."

"That's more like it." He smiled, tried to relax. Him stressing out wasn't helping her calm down. "We're gonna get through this. The house, everything will work out." He glanced over his shoulder at what used to be her home. The move had been an effort to break the tension, but if she didn't stop looking at him that way, he was going to lose his grip on that last shred of control.

"And then you'll leave again."

His heart did one of those dips and slides, all the way down to his boots. She had every right to throw that at him. "I was wrong to leave last time." He'd same as admitted that already, but this time he said the words he should have said before. "That won't happen this time until you're ready for me to go."

"You sure about that?"

"Positive."

Had she lifted her face closer to his, or was he the

one who moved? Didn't matter. All he knew for sure was that he couldn't take it anymore. He was going to kiss her, because he simply couldn't *not* kiss her. She needed it as badly as he did.

The growl of trucks roaring toward them snapped him back, mentally and physically. Her breath caught, as if she too had just been dragged away from the brink of self-indulgence. They couldn't keep dancing all around this thing between them, or they were going to lose it and go too far. Lyle had to do this right this time.

Sadie turned around just as Gus and two of his men, all three driving their big trucks, braked to a stop. Did these guys not understand the concept of conserving? One of the trucks pulled a horse trailer. Gus and the others bailed out and strode toward them.

Sadie put her hand up to shade her eyes. "Is there a horse in that trailer?"

The hope in her voice made his gut clench. "Don't think so." She was still hoping to find Dare Devil.

Lyle took a breath and braced for the battle of wills that Gus's presence unfailingly provoked. He checked the weapon at the small of his back and hoped like hell he wouldn't need to use it. It wasn't enough that Gus had been at the hospital almost as long as they had, hovering and listening. The man was worried about his daughter, for sure. But he was also trying hard to learn exactly what Lyle was up to. If he didn't already know, Lyle felt reasonably certain he had a hunch.

"What do you want?" Sadie crossed her arms over her chest. That appeared to be her standard greeting for dear old dad.

Lyle sensed that to some extent she held Gus responsible for part of this mess that was her history. She understandably felt that he should have told her at some point. In Gus's defense, how did a man tell the woman he'd raised as his own child something like that?

"I found Dare Devil."

"Where? Is he all right?"

"I don't know his status," Gus told her. "But I got word where he was being kept." He shook his head. "The Carroll place. I should've known when that old bastard started drinking again, he couldn't be trusted."

"I'll get my keys." Sadie hesitated, threw her hands up in frustration. "I can't get my keys." She turned back to the house. "They burned along with everything else I own."

"You two can ride with me," Gus offered.

Lyle slid two fingers into his pocket. "I'll drive." Gus shot him a look that declared he wasn't happy about that interception.

"I don't want you digging around in that mess, Sadie." Gus gestured to the heap that had been her house. "My men will be over tomorrow. They'll salvage what they can and bulldoze the rest." The elder Gilmore wasn't giving up on getting his daughter's attention, if not her respect.

"The insurance company is sending someone on Monday," she informed him, visibly bursting his bubble. "Professionals."

"You want strangers going through what's left of your worldly possessions, little girl?" Gus argued.

"I sure as hell don't want your *men* touching my stuff."

Sizemore, Gus's constant shadow, laughed. "You

just don't know how to be a grateful little girl, do you, Sadie Adele?"

"Shut up," Gus growled at him. "Let's go find that damned horse."

SADIE WAITED IN THE truck. Lyle had insisted. She didn't like it one bit, but she wasn't totally stupid. Her house had burned. Someone had whacked him in the head. This was not the time to be foolhardy. Her throat and nostrils were sore as hell. Her chest felt as if she'd sucked in the fire instead of just the smoke.

Gus banged on the door of the shack Jesse Carroll called home, Lyle right next to him. Sizemore and his buddy were walking the property. Sadie didn't see why they didn't go straight to the barn. If Dare Devil was here, he'd be in the barn most likely. Then again, if old man Carroll had hoped to hide him, he might do otherwise. She hugged herself, wished all of this insanity was over.

Another round of knocking on the man's door. Why didn't they just go in? Were all these guys thick-skulled?

Two more minutes passed. Finally, Gus tried the door. Evidently it was unlocked. He and Lyle went inside. Sadie sat up straighter. Lyle had left her his handgun. Her shotgun had gotten charred along with the rest of her personal possessions. She caught a glimpse of Sizemore in the woods next to the barn.

"Idiot."

Seconds ticked off like little bombs in her head. She watched the digital clock shift to the next minute and then the next and still no one came out of the house or went into the barn.

"This is ridiculous." She eyed the barn doors. Not more than fifty feet from the house, about seventy from the truck. It was broad daylight.

She was out the door and headed that way before reason could talk her out of the move. When she reached the barn, Lyle and Gus were still in the house and she had no idea where Sizemore or his pal had gotten off to. Probably relieving themselves. Cocky guys like him loved peeing in the woods.

She lifted the crossbar and the barn doors opened with a reluctant creak. It was pitch dark inside. She let the doors drift all the way open to allow as much light as possible inside. The barn smelled bad. Mr. Carroll clearly hadn't used it for much in a long time and hadn't bothered cleaning it after the last time. She eased along the main aisle, checked the six stalls, her hope withering. No Dare Devil.

There was an odd odor, besides the nasty hay and animal droppings that had petrified. The sunlight that filtered in highlighted the dust and cobwebs that had taken over. Probably spiders, too.

She turned around and retraced her steps. The tack room door stood open. She shifted directions and checked it out. It was even darker in there. She felt on the wall for a light switch. No switch. Smelled a lot worse, too. She moved to the center of the room, her right hand groping the air over her head for a pull string. Maybe there was no electricity to the barn. Had there been any overhead lights in the main area?

Her hand hit something solid. She snatched it back. Not a pull string. She squinted but still couldn't see a damned thing. Gathering her courage, she reached into the darkness again and tried to determine by touch what the object was. Fabric…then something smoother…a boot.

She stumbled back, her heart missing a beat.

A leg. She'd felt a leg.

Holding her breath, she checked to see if there were two legs. Oh, yeah. Two boots. Two legs.

Sadie backed out of the tack room, bumped the door frame on the way.

"I thought you were staying in the truck."

She jumped. Turned to face the voice. Sizemore stood in the doorway, blocking a good deal of the sun.

"There's…" She moistened her lips and reached again for her voice. "There's someone hanging in the tack room. I think it's a man. I'm pretty sure he's dead."

SHERIFF COX SHOWED UP. The coroner arrived a few minutes later. Mr. Carroll was dead. The sheriff concluded that he had hanged himself, since an overturned stepladder lay on the floor of the tack room.

Sadie didn't really know the old man. He had worked for Gus off and on in the past. He had a reputation for heavy drinking and not showing up for days. Gus had fired him a dozen times but he always took him back. Felt sorry for the old guy, she supposed. She didn't like giving him that kind of credit, but when it came to a man down on his luck, Gus wasn't completely heartless. It didn't happen often. In fact, Mr. Carroll was the only example she could think of.

A frown tugged at her brow. He'd sure as hell never offered her any credit for her good deeds.

They hadn't found Dare Devil. Apparently her father's source had been mistaken. Gus didn't like to be wrong. He'd been shouting orders, even to the sheriff for the past half hour. Now that she sat back and watched him in action, she decided that he was upset by the old man's death and this was his way of showing his emotions.

All this time she'd been certain he didn't have any. Maybe the smoke she'd sucked in had damaged her brain.

Twice Gus and Lyle had locked horns, primarily because Gus didn't like that he was here. Lyle didn't abide his intimidation tactics. Not like before.

He'd promised he wouldn't go this time until she was ready for him to leave. Could she trust his word on that?

There was no question that he would finish his job and he would protect her. But could she trust him with her heart? He'd sure stamped all over it the last time.

Her age had been a problem. She couldn't deny that. But why hadn't he written to her or called? He could have come back. But he hadn't. The ache started deep in her chest.

And here she was, risking that same kind of pain all over again.

Shouting yanked her from the troubling thoughts. Sizemore broke the tree line. He held something in his hand. Sadie felt the air rush from her lungs. She pushed off the truck and started forward.

Sizemore was leading Dare Devil.

Sadie rushed to the old horse and gave him a hug. He neighed and snorted as she quickly checked him over. Not a scratch. Her heart felt so big in her chest she couldn't possibly draw in a breath. Apparently, she had wrongly accused Gus and he had been right. That poor old man had taken her horse.

But she had him back now.

Her joy deflated as the coroner took poor old Mr. Carroll away all zipped up in a body bag.

The urge to cry came suddenly. Had that old man killed himself because he'd stolen a Gilmore horse and he didn't know how to make it right?

When had her world turned into this hurtful, scary place?

She felt like Alice after having fallen down the rabbit hole.

How did she climb out?

Her attention settled on Lyle. He was watching her. In that moment, she somehow fully understood that he was her only way out. But the path he offered would change her world again...and nothing would ever be the same.

SADIE HAULED A BUCKET of feed and water to Dare Devil's stall. She rubbed his forehead. "Glad you're home, old boy."

He ate as if he hadn't seen a bucket of feed since he was stolen. She wanted to be angry about that, but it was hard to be mad at a dead man.

Lyle joined her, gave Dare Devil a scratch behind the ears. "Gus wants us to stay at his place until we figure something out."

Sadie shot him an are-you-out-of-your-mind look. Felt bad for being obstinate, considering the small bandage covering the stitches on the back of his head.

"No," he said, reading her look accurately, "I haven't lost my mind."

"Sounds like it." She had no interest in sharing airspace with Gus for an extended period. Besides, Dare Devil deserved a good rubdown. She could use one herself. That Lyle stood so close made her shiver at the idea of him giving her a slow, attentive rubdown.

"Be reasonable, Sadie," he complained. "Sleeping in the barn until your house is rebuilt is not exactly a reasonable expectation."

"The insurance agent said they would bring me a temporary home."

"When? In a few days? Gus has that huge house and there's only him. You can't tolerate being in his presence for a few days? I'm sure you could avoid him somehow in all that space."

Sadie faced him, made sure he was paying attention. "If I take him up on his hospitality, he'll just use it against me later. I know him, Lyle. He doesn't give anything without expecting something back. I don't want to be obligated to him." She was on her own and she wanted it to stay that way.

Didn't she?

The man staring down at her made her second-guess that declaration. She had to stop doing that to herself. This was probably the worst time to even be toying with notions of their nonexistent relationship.

"What do you plan to do for basic facilities?"

She grinned. The problem had crossed her mind. "We'll go to the store and get toilet paper and hand sanitizer. There's water in here and the old outhouse still works."

He laughed. "You've got it all figured out."

"That's right." She planted her hands on her hips. "What? You all out of arguments against staying here?"

His face turned serious. "Someone burned your house down last night, with you in it. Whoever it was got the jump on me, which generally isn't an easy feat. You almost died. I don't want to take any unnecessary chances with your safety."

"But I have you to protect me," she argued, her insides melting just looking at him and how flustered he was with the whole situation. She suspected that he would prefer staying in Gus's house to being here alone with her. She had every intention of doing something about that.

"Sadie." His gaze settled on her lips. "I lost a hunk of my objectivity the moment I laid eyes on you that first morning. I've been losing ground since. I don't know if you can count on me the way you should be able to."

Just like that, she was ready to take the risk to her heart. Decision made, her arms went around his neck and she tiptoed to reach his mouth. He let her kiss him but he didn't kiss her back. So this was how it was going to be. Fine. She had promised herself that she would show him just how much of a woman she was now. She never broke a promise. Leaning into him, she deepened the kiss. He reacted. His arms wrapped around her, held her tight against him. She lifted her legs, closed them around his waist. *That felt good.*

He carried her to the stall where she'd tried to sleep the night before last and dropped to his knees. Laying her gently in the fresh hay, he smiled down at her, slowly settled his weight atop hers. Her breath hitched as heat filled her in a frantic rush. "I've waited a long time to be with you like this," he murmured.

The ability to speak eluded her for a moment. She

covered by unbuttoning his shirt. Her fingers felt clumsy. She couldn't wait to touch his bare skin. "I've dreamed of how it would be." She licked her lips. "I wanted you to be my first. Then…" She stared at her shaking fingers, tried to make them work better. "When you left I thought my life was over."

He cupped her cheek, stroked it with his thumb. "Sadie, you're so beautiful, you probably had to keep the guys off with that old shotgun of yours."

She fought the tears. Damn it, she would not cry. Not now. She wanted this moment to be special. "Occasionally."

He swiped a tear with the pad of his thumb. "Please don't cry."

She inhaled a shaky breath. "I'm sorry. It's just…" She blinked to keep more of those stupid tears back. "I don't know how to do this, Lyle. And I want to so badly."

His face darkened with confusion. "Are you saying you've never done this…you…?"

She couldn't meet his eyes. Why did they have to have this conversation? She didn't want to talk. "After you left, there wasn't anyone I wanted."

The tension that stiffened his body wasn't what she'd hoped for. "Sadie, it shouldn't be like this." He shook his head. "Not here. Definitely not a snap decision made under stressful conditions."

Her determination rallied. "Don't tell me what I want or what I should do." She yanked his shirt free of the waist of his jeans. "Stop running your mouth, McCaleb, and show me how you do this."

His mouth closed over hers, and there was no more talk. He kissed her long and deep as her hands moved over his chest, learning every ripple of muscle. The excitement and heat roared inside her. Instinctively, her body started to move against his. He groaned deep in his throat and she smiled against his lips. Oh, how she wanted this man…wanted him to teach her how to make love.

He undressed her so slowly she thought she might die before he finished. She reached for his fly, but he pushed her hands away. "I'll be right back."

Her body quivered when he left her lying there naked on the hay. Where was he going? She heard him murmuring to the dogs. The barn doors opened then closed. Suddenly he was back.

"The dogs are keeping watch outside." Hopping on one leg, he tugged off one boot, then the other. "I wasn't sure they were ready for this."

Sadie laughed. "Good thinking."

She watched, mesmerized, as he stripped off his shirt and then his jeans. Her breath stalled as his boxer briefs slid down those muscled thighs. Her eyes rounded at the sight of his aroused body.

He stretched out next to her and she gasped as that thick muscle brushed her thigh. He leaned over her and kissed her lips before making his way down to her breasts. She cried out at the feel of his mouth on her like that. The sensations were so incredible, she floated away on that delicious cloud of mindless pleasure. He touched her down there…kept teasing her until she couldn't think, then he slid one finger inside. Her body bucked. Her fingers clutched at the familiar hay.

Stretching her until two fingers fit perfectly, he delved deeper, his thumb rubbing that special place fueling all those wild sensations. He kissed and licked his way down her torso, lavished his attention on the part of her that needed more. She had to touch him. Her fingers threaded into his hair, careful of the bandage. Those bad memories tried to intrude. As if he sensed her distraction, he sat back on his knees and lifted her bottom onto his thighs, her legs spread wide and rested on each side of him. One nudge and she moaned with the shock of their most intimate places finally touching.

He gripped her bottom with one hand and guided himself into her with the other, slowly, a fraction at a time.

Sadie wanted to watch but her eyes closed as all those swirling, swelling sensations somehow curled together in one unbelievable rush. He moved in and out, an inch in, an inch out. The stretching sensation made her want to scream for more. She tried to lift into him, to take in more, but he held her back.

"Patience, baby."

The sound of his voice drifted around her, joined all those other beautiful sensations and started to build. He eased in another inch. She cried out his name. His answer was to move a little faster now, in and out.

The swell burst and showered heat over her entire body. She writhed with the pleasure of it…wanted more. Desperate to find that place again, she hurried to get her body into rhythm with his. Moving, moving, as he pushed deeper and deeper. She wasn't sure how much more pleasure she could endure.

He brought his body down on hers, filled her so completely that she couldn't breathe…couldn't speak. She could only feel. That marvelous tide started to rise again. Higher and higher until she drowned in the pull of it. His movements grew more urgent. He groaned with the effort of satisfying his own building need, and she couldn't comprehend how he had held out so long.

She felt the contractions of his orgasm even as her own muscles started that clench-and-relax rhythm all over again, squeezing the last of his climax from him.

He fell onto the hay next to her, pulling her onto her side so that their bodies remained joined.

His fingers sifted through her hair. It had come loose and was all over the place. "You okay?"

She nodded. Not sure of her voice just yet.

"Sadie…"

The worry in his eyes terrified her.

"I…"

She covered his mouth with her own, pushed him onto his back and straddled his waist. She winced as she settled down fully on him, but she knew that small discomfort would quickly pass. "I—" she decided to finish his statement for him "—want to do that again."

Chapter Thirteen

3:00 p.m.

Lyle leaned against the fence and watched the horses graze in the pasture to prevent staring at her. She had finger combed her hair and was in the process of tying it back into that haphazard ponytail that was her trademark. He'd had to bite his tongue to prevent offering to do it for her. But that would only start something he wouldn't have the willpower to stop.

His body hardened at the memory of sinking deep inside her. The ache that accompanied the memories terrified him. All this time she had waited for him, had allowed no one else to touch her the way he had longed to seven years ago. He hadn't expected that. In his mind, she had always been just out of his reach. Now he felt as if she belonged to him.

That was a dangerous position, considering he was supposed to be here to protect her. How could he do that right when she overwhelmed his senses? Blinded him to everything else?

They had talked for hours before making love again. She felt lost. Told him that she trusted nothing and no one but him. Her admission terrified him all the more. Eventually they'd washed each other with the chilly water right from the hose. Those moments had been playful and intimate, strengthening the bond that already ruled him.

Their clothes still smelled of smoke and looked somewhat worse for the wear, but that hadn't dampened their spirits in the least. A drive into town for clothes was next on his agenda. Including a food run. He was starved. She hadn't mentioned food, but she had to be famished.

When all that was done, somehow he intended to persuade her to stay at Gus's tonight. With the security at the Rocking Horse Ranch, she would be much safer. Staying here would be asking for trouble. Especially with him so far off his game.

No time like the present to approach the subject. "I was thinking—"

"I'm not changing my mind about Gus's offer."

She'd cut him off before he'd started. "Sadie, be reasonable. The security is impenetrable. Safety has to be our top priority. Dare Devil is back and that threat isn't likely to be repeated."

Frustration lined her brow as she glared at him with an unrelenting determination. "Not happening, so let it go. I'm not going to put myself at his mercy. Not today. Not tomorrow. Not any day."

Well, damn. "You are one hardheaded woman, Sadie Adele."

"That's what they tell me." She slipped between the fence rails and loped out to frolic with the horses.

What the hell was he going to do with the woman? She refused to listen to reason. He could hog-tie her and take the decision out of her hands. Then Gus would jump him the way he had Sizemore for making a stupid comment.

There was no way to win here.

His cell vibrated. He dragged it from his pocket and checked the screen. Not a number he recognized. That could be good or bad. "McCaleb."

Two seconds into the conversation he understood the news wasn't good. Lyle pocketed his phone and wondered how to break this to Sadie. She didn't need any more pain and stress. He ducked under the top rail and joined her in the pasture. This was something he couldn't protect her from.

She studied his face as he approached and then frowned. "What?"

Apparently he'd completely lost his ability to conceal his feelings. "Gus was in an accident. He's at the hospital. He's pretty banged up, Sadie, but he's stable. They're going to keep him for a while just to make sure." He heaved a burdened breath. "He's asking for you."

The sun-warmed color had faded from her face as he'd spoken. "Take me to him."

HE TRIED TO REASSURE her on the way into town. She said nothing, just stared out at the passing landscape. How much was one woman supposed to take? He hadn't been able to protect her from the pain of any of this. Every aspect of the situation just kept escalating further and further out of control.

She was opening her door before the truck was in Park. He shut off the engine and rushed to catch up with her. The lobby was deserted except for the woman behind the information desk. Sadie stormed her position.

"Gus Gilmore," she announced. "Where is he?"

So much for decorum. "We got a call that he'd been in an accident," Lyle explained.

The woman checked her computer. "Third floor." She looked up and offered a sympathetic smile. "Room 311."

Sadie headed for the elevator.

"Thank you." Lyle gave the woman a nod and rushed to catch up with Sadie. The elevator doors closed as he slid inside. "You need to take a breath before you see him."

"I know what I need to do." Her hands were pushed deep into the pockets of her jeans, as if she were a kid about to enter the principal's office. "I don't know why you insist on telling me what to do." The elevator bumped to a stop and the doors slid open. "You're as bad as Gus."

Lyle let her remark roll off his back. She was protecting herself from yet another harsh reality that had invaded her life. She couldn't be soft and sweet right now. If she allowed that vulnerability, she would be shattered.

SADIE PUSHED THE DOOR inward and walked into the room. What the hell had the old man gotten himself into this time? He lay too still in the bed. His face was battered and swollen, the skin an angry red against the stark white canvas of the bed linens. Her knees betrayed her. Lyle served as her buoy and steadied her.

The heart monitor beeped the same slow, steady tempo as the one she remembered from her mother's hospital room and then her grandmother's. The wavy lines that accompanied the sound didn't seem nearly bright and strong enough, but she had no idea what that meant. An IV line dangled from a bag and attached to his arm. When there was nothing else to distract herself with she looked at him again. He wasn't the strong, mean man she fought with most every day. He was small and weak, and that scared her to death.

"Where'd you get your driver's license?" she asked as she moved to his bedside. "A Cracker Jack box?"

His lids fluttered open and he stared up at her, his eyes bloodshot and puffy. He made a grumbling sound meant to be a laugh. "I know for a fact that's where you got yours."

The air wouldn't fill her lungs and that damned stinging was back in her eyes. "What do you expect? Look who I had for a teacher." At first it had been a tractor, twisting and turning all around the fields. Then that damned old truck of her grandfather's, the same one she still drove. Gus had sworn she'd never make it through the driver's test driving that way.

Gus closed his eyes. "I guess you're right about that."

She braced her hands on the bed rail. "So what happened, old man? Whatever it was you look like you got the short end of the stick."

"I don't know." He blinked a few times then stared at the ceiling instead of meeting her gaze. "Some fool ran me off the road. Probably texting and driving. You young folks don't have a lick of sense."

"You break anything?" She didn't see any sign of a cast or sling.

"Few cracked ribs," he said nonchalantly. "Got

myself a concussion. They're keeping an eye on my spleen." He cleared his throat. "Nothing that won't heal or that I can't live without."

"That's good to hear." He was in a lot of pain, she could tell. That crazy shaking started deep in her bones.

He reached out to the railing, covered her hand with his. It felt cold and rough, but familiar and comforting. Those damned tears wouldn't stay back.

"I told them not to bring me here, that I'd be fine, but you know how they can be." He grunted another pained laugh. "They just want my money. I've got their number."

Sadie produced a smile and nodded. "Most people do."

He chuckled. "Yeah, I guess so."

No crying. She didn't dare say anything else. Her entire powers of concentration were necessary to keep her emotions beat back and to stay vertical.

"Get around here where I can see you, McCaleb."

Lyle did as he asked, standing beside Sadie. She was so damned glad he was here. There were so many questions to which she wanted to demand answers. How could she do that with Gus in this condition?

Gus fixed his attention on Lyle. "I know why you came here."

"We don't have to talk about that now, Mr. Gilmore. You need to save your strength. Focus on recovering."

"To hell you say. I've ignored the situation too long already."

A new wave of anticipation charged through Sadie. She wanted him to make her understand how all this happened—if it was true even though she knew it was. She held her tongue for fear of stopping him. She wanted him to make it all right, as he did when she skinned her knee as a little girl, long before her mother died.

"That woman, Clare Barker, called me the night she was released. Crazy bitch."

The impact of his announcement shook Sadie hard. It was true. Dear God. She had known. She had. But hearing it from her father somehow made it more real. She hadn't wanted it to be true.

"Said she was coming for her baby girl. I told her to go to hell. I had my men watching Sadie before you got here, McCaleb, so don't think you got the jump on me."

"Course not, Mr. Gilmore. I'm very much aware of how much you love your daughter. You made that very clear a long time ago."

"Yeah, well, that's another story for another time."

Sadie's brain couldn't keep up with the dozens of thoughts and memories and theories spiraling there. She didn't want to hear this. She had thought she did, but she had been wrong. Gus Gilmore taught her how to ride a horse and then a bike. How to drive…how to run a ranch. It didn't matter that he wasn't the man who contributed to her DNA, he was her father. Nothing would ever change that. Those hot, salty tears she'd been trying to hold back streamed down her cheeks, and she silently cursed herself for the weakness.

"It was your momma." Gus's full attention settled on Sadie then. "She got cancer a few years after we married and they had to take everything to save her." He made a face that said that loss was irrelevant to him. "I didn't care, as long as she was okay. I just didn't want to lose her. But the idea that she couldn't have children ate at her just like that damned cancer they cut out of her. There was nothing I could do to make her happy. She was just plain miserable. I wasn't always the perfect husband. I made mistakes. But I knew if I could just find a way to fix things for her, she would be happy. Nothing else in this world mattered to me."

"She never told me about the first cancer." Sadie hated the wobble in her voice. She wanted to be strong. This was all so confusing.

"It was a hard time for us both." Gus found that place on the ceiling again, avoiding eye contact. "We kept to ourselves, too broken to be social. The ranch became our refuge. We didn't have to see anybody, didn't have to talk about it. But I knew that wouldn't last forever. Eventually we'd have to deal with the issue."

Sadie tried her best to prepare for what came next. Lyle placed his hand at the small of her back. It was all she could do to keep from throwing herself against his chest and sobbing like a child.

"I talked to a friend of mine up in Austin. He was one of those fancy lawyers you know would do most anything for money." Gus fiddled with the sheet with his free hand and kept the other one clasped tightly over Sadie's. "I didn't care. I just wanted him to fix this for us. I told him what I needed and how much I'd pay. Six months later he called me and said he had a little girl who needed a home. He took care of all the paperwork and I gave him the cash."

"Mr. Gilmore," Lyle said quietly, "do you have any idea who was on the other side of that deal."

"My friend," Gus went on as if Lyle hadn't said a

word, "he'd made a reputation for himself in Austin. Folks knew who to go to without having to worry about it making the news or hitting the police's radar. He said the woman called him with three little girls who needed good homes. He wasn't a fool any more than I was. It was all over the news, the papers. We both knew where they'd come from, but neither one of us cared."

"Did you meet this woman?"

Sadie felt Lyle's tension mounting almost as fast as hers.

"I did not." He looked directly at Lyle then. "But her name was Janet or Janice, that I know for sure." He turned to Sadie, his eyes watery with emotion. "I knew you were sisters. I tried to get all three of you, but the lawyer said that was impossible. He wouldn't accept any offer I made. I figure he was trying to protect you from being discovered. Or maybe himself. The law was looking for three little girls, not one."

"Can you give me the attorney's name?" Lyle asked.

"Wouldn't matter. He died eight or ten years ago. I saw his obit in the newspaper. Fact is, I don't think he knew any more than I did. This Janet or Janice was smart. She wasn't about to get caught."

"You never heard from her or the attorney again?"

"Nope. Not after we picked up Sadie, along with a few baby photos." He chuckled softly. "She was the prettiest little thing in that fancy dress they stuck on her. She kept pulling at it, trying to get it off. I knew she was going to be a handful."

Gus turned to Sadie. She tried to smile but she had gone numb about two questions ago. She couldn't conceive the proper words to say.

"I'm sorry, little girl. I should have told you a long

time ago, but I couldn't bring myself to do it. After your mother died I was scared to death of losing you, too." Tears leaked from the corners of his eyes. In her whole life, she had never seen her father cry. "I guess I managed to do that anyway."

Pride and affection burst inside Sadie. "What're you talking about, old man? I'm here, aren't I? You think I don't have better things to do?" She leaned down and kissed his bruised cheek. "I love you, Daddy," she whispered. "I always have."

They cried together for a while. Sadie knew it was time to go. He needed his rest and this emotional exchange had taken a toll. She promised to be back soon. And Gus made Lyle vow that he would keep her safe or die trying. Lyle gave his word without hesitation. Sadie could have sworn his eyes looked a little watery, too.

Outside the room, Sizemore and Radley waited on opposite sides of her father's door. "Cox is looking for the two of you," Sizemore said with a sneer.

God, Sadie despised the man. "Good for him." Sizemore wasn't worth the energy required to get angry. Cox, either, for that matter.

Lyle kept his arm around her shoulder as they moved through the hospital. Sadie felt some sense of relief. A truckload of sadness. And determination. But relief to understand how this happened. This woman, Clare Barker, was not going to destroy her family. Whatever happened twenty-two years ago was way, way over now. Sadie was a Gilmore, and by God no one was going to change that.

Sadie leaned into Lyle. He and the Colby Agency would find a way to stop this insanity. She was safe with him.

They had reached the parking lot before running into the sheriff. He waited at Lyle's truck.

"Sadie." He nodded at her. To Lyle he said, "We have a little problem."

She rolled her eyes. What now?

"That vehicle that ran your daddy off the road was a truck," the sheriff informed them.

"Is that why you've been inspecting *my* truck?" Lyle asked pointedly.

Sheriff Cox nodded. "I also sent one of my deputies to take a look at your truck, Sadie."

All those painful emotions that had been tearing at her since she'd heard that Gus was in the hospital coalesced into one—outrage. "What the hell are you talking about?"

"Seeing how you and your daddy have been at odds for a good long while now and you've publicly threatened him several times, I would have been remiss not to follow that lead."

"Are you that inept, Cox," Lyle blasted him, "or just desperate for a big payoff from whoever put that crazy notion in your head?"

Cox got in Lyle's face. "I don't care who you work for, McCaleb, I will arrest you and then you can have all the time you want in jail to think of a way to get back in my good graces."

Sadie put her hand on Lyle's arm. "The sheriff's right. He's only doing his job."

Lyle didn't want to let it go so easily, but he backed off when Sadie sent another silent plea his way with her eyes. She had had enough and so had he.

"Your truck," Cox said to her, "has damage on the

driver's side consistent with the kind of ramming strategy that sent your daddy practically to his death."

"I haven't driven my truck in the last twenty-four hours, Sheriff Cox. If someone else did, then you'll just have to haul her in and find their fingerprints. But it wasn't me." She was proud of herself for remaining calm enough to make the statement in a reasonable tone.

"What time did the accident occur?" Lyle asked.

"'Bout two o'clock as best we can assess."

"Today?" Lyle persisted. "As in p.m.?"

Sadie stared at him in confusion. Why would he ask that? They had followed Gus in his truck to the Carroll place this morning before noon. The sheriff had been there, too, as a matter of fact. He knew it had to be p.m., probably while they were making love in the barn.

"You know that's what I mean," Cox fired back.

"That's what I thought." Lyle braced his hands on his hips. "And you're fully aware that Sadie's house burned down last night. You were there."

"That's right," Cox agreed. "If she thinks Gus had anything to do with that, the fire is just additional motive, not an alibi."

Sadie's cool started seeping from her grasp. How dare this knucklehead make such an accusation! Yes, she and Gus didn't get along the better part of the time, but that didn't mean she wanted to hurt him.

"Then why don't you tell me how she drove her truck when the keys went up in flames along with the rest of her stuff?"

Cox was dumbfounded for about three seconds. Long enough for Lyle to toss in, "If you'll read your deputy's report, I stated that when I was ambushed I was inspecting damage to the front driver's side of Sadie's truck. What're you going to call that? Premeditation?"

Cox hitched up his trousers. "I'll be looking into that."

"Good," Lyle groused.

Leaving the sheriff standing there staring after them, Sadie and Lyle loaded into his truck.

"That's what's wrong with this town," he growled as he started the engine, then backed out of the parking slot.

Sadie looked from him to Cox and back. His frustration planted a tiny seed of hope in her heart. "Oh, yeah?"

"Yeah." He drove away from the frustration. "You need a decent sheriff."

Her biological mother was out there somewhere trying to get to her daughters. The man who had been her father her whole life had almost been killed in an accident with which the sheriff thought she was involved. Even with all that going down, she leaned back in the seat and felt a sense of optimism for the first time in days. "I guess we do."

As foolish as hanging on to the idea that he might actually stay was, she needed something to cling to if she was going to get through this.

Chapter Fourteen

Victoria waited as patiently as possible. Warden Prentice was not happy that she asked for this meeting. He asserted, and rightly so, that each time she was logged in as a visitor he ran the risk of a leak to the media. The press was already sniffing around with regard to the coming execution of the Princess Killer.

But this would not wait. Clare Barker had vanished. There had to be some aspect of her past that would provide a clue to where she would go or to the identity of this one-armed man who had facilitated her vanishing act.

There was no one else to ask. She had no other family and no friends that they were aware of. Whatever Barker could offer might prove useful. He was all they had.

The door opened and Barker was escorted inside by two guards. The usual precautions were taken once he was seated. This time he made eye contact with Victoria the instant he was settled at the interview table.

When the door had closed behind the guards, he asked, "You found my daughters?"

Any sympathy the man had garnered from her on that first visit was gone now. She had concrete reasons not to trust anything he told her. "Janet Tolliver is dead."

He nodded, his expression one of sadness. "I was told."

Anger stirred. Was that all he could say? Victoria restrained the urge to demand answers. "How did she know we were coming?"

The hint of anger that surfaced in her voice had Barker searching her face and eyes. "She would never have entrusted you with the information she had if I hadn't sent word to her."

"So this contact you have developed is so loyal that you don't question how your requests are carried out."

He shook his head, going on the defensive now. "I don't understand what you're getting at. Obviously, you received the evidence, which means Janet must have been alive after my contact passed along the message."

Victoria leaned forward, looked him square in the eyes. "Someone violently murdered her, Mr. Barker. Who else besides you knew she had that evidence?"

"No one."

"Not your connection?"

He shook his head. "Of course not. He only carried the message. *Expect someone from the Colby Agency.*"

Victoria narrowed her gaze and searched his as carefully as he had examined hers. "You don't seem upset that your friend died to protect your secret."

All emotion, even the guarded expression that had gone up as a defense mechanism, disappeared. "I appreciate what you're doing to protect my daughters. There is no way I can hope to repay you. But it feels as if you're accusing me of something, and I don't understand why. I've done nothing but try to ensure my daughters were protected."

The man was good, she would give him that. But not good enough. She had spent some time with the warden before this meeting. He had identified the one-armed man. A nurse in the infirmary, Tony Weeden, had provided medical care for Rafe Barker's allergy-related asthma condition for the past three years. Tony had lost his right arm in an accident as a young boy. His height and hair color matched those of the man who had whisked Clare Barker away. Not to mention the apartment next to hers had been rented under the name Toni Westen. Seemed a little coincidental now that they had the one-armed man's name, though he had not been seen going in or out of the apartment since Clare's arrival next door. He had facilitated her escape. The means had been planned for months.

"Mr. Barker, I warned you from the beginning that unless you were truthful with me, my agency could not help you." He had fallen well short of that single standard.

He shook his head. "I wish you would simply explain what it is you believe I've done."

Victoria tamped back the anger and impatience. "Clare Barker has vanished. Our surveillance ended abruptly after her apartment complex was destroyed by a fire that has been ruled as arson."

"She started this fire? Was anyone killed?"

"No lives were lost, thankfully. We don't believe she started the fire. There is reason to suspect her accomplice used the fire as a distraction to facilitate her getaway."

Barker sighed. Gave a little shrug. "I'm not surprised she has made friends to help her. She is as desperate as I am, only for different reasons."

"There's just one thing." Victoria watched closely in hopes of catching some small reaction besides this annoying nonchalance and indifference. "You seem to have at least one mutual friend."

"That's impossible." A spark of outrage appeared in his eyes.

Victoria nodded resolutely. "Your nurse at the infirmary. Tony Weeden. He was her accomplice. We have the two of them on video leaving the scene together."

"I don't believe you."

There it was. Shock. Disbelief. If Barker had any idea that Weeden and Clare were associates, he did an award-winning job of covering it up.

Victoria reached into the bag the guards had allowed her to bring into the room and removed the photo she'd had printed from a single frame of the video. She placed the glossy enlarged shot on the table. "You're saying that is not Tony Weeden."

Barker stared at the photograph for an extended period. It occurred to Victoria that this might be the first image he had seen of his wife in about twenty years. Would that prompt him to tell the truth, or would seeing her free with his friend fuel a rage that would end his cooperation?

"That is Tony." His tone was blank, low, almost a whisper.

"Then you see how I might suspect you're not being completely honest with me."

"I don't understand why he would do this." Barker

shook his head again. "I thought he was my friend. That he believed in my innocence."

"Does he have information that could prove detrimental to our investigation and how we protect your daughters?" The answer was essential to getting the job done.

"He knows very little. As you are aware, until I sent you that letter I rarely spoke to anyone, verbally or otherwise."

"But he knows something," she pressed.

"He knows I'm innocent and that the girls are alive. He passed the word to Janet that you were coming. That's all."

That was enough. "Is he capable of murder, in your opinion?"

He considered the question for a time. "I would say no, but obviously I am not a good judge of character. I believed he sincerely wanted to help me and was loyal to the cause."

"Is he the one who mailed the letter you sent me?"

"Yes. He read it and insisted on helping me." Rafe looked away as if attempting to regain his composure. "Why would he do this? Surely he understood there would be consequences."

"Only if we can find him."

"He works here every day. He never misses a day."

"He didn't show up for his shift today. He isn't answering his phone and his neighbors haven't seen him in two days. He's not coming back, Mr. Barker. And unless we can find the two of them, my investigators will have no choice but to work in a reactive state under the assumption that both Tony and Clare represent a threat to our clients."

Barker stared at her, blinked.

"Do you understand what that means, Mr. Barker?"

He blinked a second time.

"Shoot to kill, Mr. Barker, that's what it means."

Barker was taken from the interview room five minutes later without having uttered another word.

He knew something or was planning something. Victoria felt it in the most basic minerals of her bones. Either way, the stakes were upped.

These women were in extreme danger. The Colby Agency would do whatever necessary to protect them.

Chapter Fifteen

Second Chance Ranch, 8:30 p.m.

Sheriff Cox ordered two of his deputies and a tow truck to take Sadie's truck away. Not one word Lyle said to the guy had penetrated that thick skull of his. He just kept repeating that same mantra. *I have a job to do.* The strangest part was the idea that Gus would not want him to do this.

Since when did Cox ignore the desires of Gus Gilmore? He'd lived comfortably in the man's hip pocket for decades now. Didn't make a whole lot of sense. It also didn't make him the kind of bad guy who would go to these extremes.

After the deputies had gone, Sadie stood there in the moonlight staring at the charred rubble that had been her home. He wished there was more he could do or say. The promise that this would pass in time just wasn't enough.

Lyle strode over to where she stood. "The horses are tucked in for the night. So are the dogs. Can I convince you to go to a hotel with me?" Sounded like a bad pickup line.

"I don't know about leaving them."

Her hesitation was understandable. "How about a nice, relaxing dinner before we hit the hay then?"

She smiled.

He tucked a strand of hair behind her ear. "That's what I like to see." His chest tightened with the need to hold her and promise her anything she wanted to hear.

"You think he'll be okay?"

Her father's condition was part of the burden weighing down those slender shoulders. Lyle wrapped his arm around her and pulled her close, urged her to lean on him. "The doctor said he's doing fine. He'll be home tomorrow. You'll see."

She shuddered with the release of a heavy breath. "He looked so old and fragile in that bed."

"He's tough," Lyle assured her. "A lot tougher than the truck he was driving." According to the sheriff the truck was totaled. Whoever ran him off the road knew exactly where to strike. Gus never saw the other vehicle. He was making that left turn and suddenly he had overshot the turn and was barreling into the ravine.

It was a flat-out miracle he survived. If Sadie were herself, she'd swear he was too mean to die.

But she wasn't herself by a long shot. If he were in her shoes, Lyle couldn't say he would fare any better.

"Okay." She turned to him, tilted that pretty face up to his. "How about that dinner?"

He pressed a kiss to her forehead and guided her to his truck. The sooner he had her out of here, the happier he would be. After Victoria's report on her last meeting with Rafe Barker, Lyle had a bad feeling that the situation was about to deteriorate fast.

SADIE WASN'T HUNGRY but Lyle had insisted she order. She played with the straw in her water glass, wished it was a beer. Thing was, she rarely drank beer or wine, not since her teenage days anyway. But right now seemed like a good time for one or two. Too much was going on to allow her senses to be dulled. The hospital could call. She'd spoken to Gus a couple of hours ago, but that didn't keep her from worrying. Her father had always been strong, immortal almost.

"Penny for your thoughts."

Somehow she pushed a smile into place for her dinner companion and bodyguard. He deserved all the smiles she could summon. If he hadn't been here…

"I was thinking about Gus. At my mother's funeral he was so solemn and hard looking. He didn't cry. Shook hands and chatted with his friends." Sadie let those memories she usually repressed play out in her mind. "I hated him for that. Then when his own mother died…he was the same way. Like it didn't matter. Just business as usual."

"You were young, Sadie. It's difficult to understand the way some handle emotion."

"I spent most of my life thinking he didn't love me, he loved *controlling* me."

"You're a lot like him."

Sadie didn't know what to make of that. She shook her head. "Seriously, you're kidding, right?"

He laughed that rumbling sound that made her shiver. She'd forgotten how sexy his laugh was. They'd certainly had nothing much to laugh about since he came back.

"Well, let's see." He leaned his elbows on the table and ticked off the similarities on his fingers. "You're both as stubborn as hell. Refuse to give an inch in battle. And you both love your horses."

She waved her hands in his face. "Wait, wait, wait. He doesn't love those animals the way I do." No way. Her father was too driven. He expected the animals to be just as driven, no matter how old and worn out they were.

"Think about it, Sadie. Have you ever actually seen him mistreat an animal?" Before she could argue, he added, "I mean the way some of the other rodeo kings do?"

Well, he had her there. "I guess not."

Lyle raised his hands in the air as if he'd just gone way over the necessary eight seconds. "It's a miracle. You admitted you might be wrong."

She laughed, couldn't help herself.

"Gus just has different expectations and standards. That's all. The same way he had expectations for you."

Sadie flatted her hands on the table and stared at the finger that still had no ring. Yeah, she was young, but she'd been in love with the same guy for her whole adult life. Didn't that count? "He made you leave."

Lyle placed his hands over hers. "He suggested I leave. I left because it was the right thing to do at the time."

She lifted her gaze to his. "You wanted to go?" Of course he had. Just because they'd made love this morning didn't mean he loved her…that he'd ever loved her.

"You were fifteen," he reminded her as if she could have forgotten. "You had a right to be who you were going to be without me taking that away from you before you were old enough to have a clue."

She pulled her hands free of his and leaned as far back in the booth as the padded fake leather upholstery would allow. The disappointment in his blues eyes almost stopped her from saying what she needed to say. "I kept thinking you'd call or come back to get me." The admission hurt even now, seven years later.

"I did call." He held her gaze, didn't cut her any slack. "On your eighteenth birthday. You were in Cancún or some place. I left a message. Sent you a card."

He called. Sent her a card? "I didn't know." She shook her head. If her daddy wasn't half-dead, she'd kill him. "Gus told me you'd moved to California and had a wife."

Lyle scrubbed a hand over his unshaved jaw. At least something good came of the fire. He hadn't been able to shave. Inside, she quivered at the remembered feel of that stubbled jaw caressing her skin.

"Well, I did spend a little time in California, but there was no woman."

"But you've had girlfriends." Sadie wanted to slither under the table. How could she have said that?

He shrugged. "No girlfriend really. A few dates." He hesitated a moment. "If you're asking me if I've been celibate this whole time, the answer is no."

That hurt. She couldn't pretend otherwise.

"If what you want to know," he offered, "is if I have ever wanted anyone the way I wanted you, that answer is no, as well."

Her heart launched into a crazy staccato. "You said *wanted,* as in past tense."

The sweetest, sexiest smile she had ever seen broke across his lips. "You didn't feel my answer to that this morning?"

Heat rushed across her cheeks. "You made your point."

He leaned close. "If that waitress ever brings our food, I'm thinking we should go to Gus's house and try out that cute canopy bed you told me you had in your room."

Donning a properly affronted face, she declared, "You cad."

Their waitress arrived before he could defend himself. When she arranged their entrées on the table and hurried away, Sadie leaned toward him and whispered, "You take me back to the barn for a few hours and I promise we'll spend the rest of the night at the mansion."

He licked his lips, whether from her offer or from the heavenly aroma of the food steaming between them she couldn't say. As if he'd read her mind, he said, "Deal."

"I THOUGHT YOU SAID you weren't really hungry," Lyle teased as he drove along her driveway, the headlamps highlighting the massive pile of rubble that had been her home.

Sadie flattened her hand on her tummy. "I think I might die. You shouldn't have let me eat so much."

"Hey. I was just glad you left the plate."

"Funny."

She was out of the truck by the time he'd grabbed his weapon and the take-home bag from the restaurant and rounded the hood. She closed the door and leaned against it. "I'm not sure I can move."

Lyle swept her into his arms and started for the barn. "Don't worry, I'll do all the moving."

She banged on his chest. "You are not funny."

He sat her down long enough to open the barn doors and turn on the light. The dogs jumped around in a little dance accompanied by their yapping.

He turned back to Sadie. "One moment."

She made a face. "Hurry up!"

Grabbing a blanket, he hustled to that last stall. After fluffing the hay, he spread the blanket over it and tried to slow the need building to a frenzy inside him. He wanted this time to be slow and awesome. This morning he hadn't been able to hold out as long as he'd hoped to. He tucked his weapon beneath the hay. No need to remind her of the troubles still hanging over their heads.

The horses shuffled around in their stalls as he dashed back to the front of the barn. "Ready."

She strolled past him. Lyle herded the dogs outside and gave them the treat he'd brought from the restaurant. With them occupied, he closed the barn doors and hurried back to where Sadie waited.

He came to an abrupt stop. She had shed her boots and clothes, everything but those cute little pink panties and the matching bra she'd bought while they were in town today.

"Wow." She was way ahead of him...but he was catching up entirely too fast.

She crooked her finger at him. "Come on, cowboy. Let's see what you've got."

The boots came off first. Sadie taunted him into making a show of the rest. He opened his fly and lowered the zipper really slowly. She urged him on, and he refused to disappoint her. By the time he was on the blanket with her, he was more than ready.

Using all the restraint he could muster, he made love to her the way she deserved. He showed her with his every kiss how very much he cared, how much he had missed her and all that he hoped for in the future.

Their future.

She showed him that she was no little girl anymore. She was all woman and she wanted him to acknowledge that. He did his best to do just that. He took great pleasure in acknowledging every womanly part of her over and over again.

Rocking Horse Ranch, May 24, 1:00 a.m.

"THIS IS STRANGE." Sadie leaned forward. "Where is everyone?" The house was darker than the night, not a single light on inside. Even the outside lights were off. Couldn't be a power outage. Gus had a whole-house generator.

"Should we check the bunkhouse? Sizemore and his playmates should be around somewhere."

"Good idea." Sadie didn't like this. With Gus in the hospital, Sizemore was supposed to be in charge. Looked as if he had fallen down on the job.

Lyle drove to the bunkhouse. No lights there, either. He handed her his cell. "Stay here. Lock the doors. Anything happens, get down and call 911."

Sadie hit the lock button as soon as he was out of the vehicle. This was too weird. Something was really wrong. She entered the number on her cell for the hospital and got the nurse's desk on her father's floor. He was sleeping comfortably. Sadie hugged herself, the phone in hand, and tried to see any movement around the bunkhouse. Lyle had gone inside already. The headlights split the night, their beam spreading wide on each side of the truck.

Lyle exited the bunkhouse and started back to the truck. She hit the unlock button so he could open the door. "Did you talk to anyone?"

He slid behind the wheel and shifted into Drive. He met her expectant gaze then. "There's no one in the bunkhouse."

Fear infused her blood. "Maybe…maybe they're in town partying since the boss is out of commission."

"Maybe."

Lyle drove back to the house. Her nerves jangled when he hit the brakes next to the dark house. This was just creepy.

"I need to go in there," he said, "but I don't know about taking you inside, and I can't leave you out here."

Sadie had grown up in this house. She knew the place. There was probably a perfectly reasonable explanation for all of this. Sizemore was likely exercising his newly found power.

"I'm calling Cox." Lyle reached for his phone.

"Let's just go in." They were making too much of this. She reached for her door.

Lyle grabbed her other hand. "Listen to me, Sadie."

The urgency in his voice had that trickle of fear breaking into a raging river.

"You stay behind me. Don't make a sound." He gave the phone back to her. "If we run into trouble, you run, hide, whichever is handiest, and you call for help."

"Okay."

He was out before her. He closed his door silently, so she did the same. Her heart was thumping wildly. Lyle moved up the steps, she followed. She hoped Gus hadn't changed his security code. Otherwise Sheriff Cox would have another reason to suspect Sadie of criminal activity.

Lyle had her stand to one side while he opened the door. It wasn't locked and the security system's warning remained silent. Another wave of intense fear rushed through her veins. She should have let him call the sheriff.

The house was eerily quiet. Lyle closed the door behind her and stopped her when she reached for the light. He clicked on the flashlight she hadn't realized he'd grabbed from the truck. The beam flowed over the shiny marble floor of the massive entry hall. They moved from room to room, Sadie right behind him, clutching the back of his shirt.

When they reached Gus's study, Sadie gasped. The room had been torn apart. "Oh, my God."

"Don't touch anything, Sadie."

She pressed her fist to her lips and bit down to hold back the hysteria. What happened here? A robbery? That didn't explain the absence of all the ranch hands.

Would Clare Barker do this? "Could it be *her?*"

Lyle moved back into the hall. "I don't know, but we're not taking any chances." He reached for the phone. "I'm calling Cox."

"No need to call the sheriff."

Sadie almost jumped out of her skin. She turned toward the voice. Billy Sizemore. She blinked and stared again at his image in the flashlight's beam. He had a gun...*pointed at them.*

"He's on his way," Billy announced. "But he'll be too late to do you two any good."

Lyle moved in front of Sadie. "What's this about, Sizemore?"

"It's about proving to Gus Gilmore that I'm the only heir he needs."

"What?" Sadie tried to move around Lyle, but he held her back. "Have you lost your mind?"

"Oh," Sizemore said with a cruel smirk, "I guess you didn't know he's my daddy. My *real* daddy. Seems like there's a lot he forgot to tell you about."

I wasn't always the perfect husband. Sadie felt light-headed. *No.* She had to keep it together. No way was she going to let this cocky SOB get away with this.

"You've been blackmailing him."

Sadie turned to Lyle. Was he guessing? Did he know something about this?

Sizemore laughed. "I didn't have to blackmail him." His expression darkened. "At least not at first. He said I was the best bronc rider he'd ever seen." Fury tightened his voice. "But that wasn't enough when I told him that little affair he had while his wife was sick was no longer in his past. He didn't like it. Seemed he already had one secret too many."

Sadie tried to push past Lyle, but again he held her back. She shouted over his shoulder, "So you tried to kill him and make it look like I did it? You bastard!"

"The whole town knows you two do nothing but fight. When they find out I caught you breaking into the house, they won't be surprised. It was dark, I didn't know it was you when I fired my weapon. Your boyfriend here fired the first shot, started a domino effect, so to speak."

"You got it all figured out," Lyle said quietly. "Stole Dare Devil to get Sadie fired up."

"Worked, didn't it? She came over here waving that shotgun of hers around."

"Too bad you had to kill old man Carroll to keep him quiet."

Lyle's suggestion sent Sadie's breath rushing from her lungs. "How could you kill a helpless old man like that?"

Sizemore laughed. "He was dead anyway. Cirrhosis."

"Guess your plan worked," Lyle offered.

"Like a charm," Sizemore bragged.

Lyle shoved Sadie to the floor.

Shots fired, the sound echoing off the walls.

The flashlight hit the floor and the beam bounced around the room.

For two seconds Sadie couldn't move. Where was Lyle? Why was it so quiet? She started to get up. A second round of shots shattered the silence. She scooted deeper into the doorway of her father's study.

Someone groaned.

Lyle? She wanted to call out to him…but what if he was down…

The chandelier came on. Light glittered across the shiny marble.

She blinked to force her eyes to focus. Lyle stood over Sizemore, the muzzle of his weapon shoved into the bastard's skull. "Slide your weapon across the floor, Sizemore."

He hesitated but then did as he was told.

That was when Sadie saw the blood splatted on

the marble. Sizemore had caught a bullet in his right leg. Blood soaked into the denim.

Sadie scrambled to her feet, ignoring the ongoing conversation between Lyle and that idiot on the floor. She stared at the splatters. Visually traced the trail. Lyle's free hand was pressed against his side. Blood seeped around and between his fingers.

Oh, God.

She rushed to his side. "You're bleeding."

He flashed a weak smile. "It's not as bad as it looks."

"Where's the phone?" She spotted it near where he'd first shoved her out of danger's path. Almost falling in her haste, she snatched up the phone and entered 911.

Blue lights flashed outside. How? She was confused. Wait, Sizemore had said the sheriff was on his way. The dispatcher came on the line. Sadie pleaded for an ambulance to be sent right away. The dispatcher assured her that one was on the way. Since Sheriff Cox had arrived it wasn't necessary for her to remain on the line.

The sheriff cuffed Sizemore and his deputies took control of all the weapons, including Lyle's. Sadie felt helpless, frantic and exhausted all at the same time. Lyle just kept explaining what happened to the sheriff while his shirt soaked up the blood seeping from his wound.

By the time the ambulance arrived she felt near cardiac arrest. Lyle refused to get in the ambulance unless Sadie could ride in the back with him.

When the doors closed and they were on their way with a paramedic seeing to his wound, she fell apart.

She hated the weakness. But she was entitled. Her world had already fallen apart.

4:00 a.m.

SIMON RUHL HAD ARRIVED to take up Lyle's slack since he was injured and the extent of treatment was not known when Lyle made the call en route to the hospital. At the hospital, Sadie refused to leave his side. The bullet had made a clean exit and surgery wasn't required. Just some cleanup work and closure.

Gus had appeared, much to the dismay of the nurses on the third floor since he had no business being out of bed. Between Gus, the sheriff and what Sizemore had told Lyle and Sadie, they had his story whether he officially confessed or not.

The sheriff had taken Sadie's truck in because both he and Gus suspected Sizemore was behind his accident as well as Dare Devil's abduction.

Sizemore had overheard Gus's conversation with Clare Barker, so he had known what was going down with Sadie. But so far he had not admitted to burning down the house or leaving the message on Sadie's door.

Gus, clad in his boots and a hospital gown, stood at the end of Lyle's bed looking far more like hell than Lyle. Sadie stood at Lyle's bedside, his hand clutched in hers.

Funny, in a million years he would never have imagined this scene. Lyle had to laugh.

Gus glared at him. "Boy, I don't know what you've got to laugh about, so I'm going to assume they're giving you better drugs than they're giving me."

Sadie laughed then, too. Once she started, she didn't seem to be able to stop. The hysteria proved contagious. Gus Gilmore laughed so hard he had to hold his damaged ribs.

When they had caught their collective breath, Gus shuffled over to Sadie and kissed her on the cheek. "I gotta get back to my room."

She smiled and gave him a nod.

Lyle had already seen the turning point. These two were going to be okay.

"Gus," she called out to him before he got out the door. He turned back to her and raised his eyebrows in expectation. "I love you."

"Course you do. And I love you."

The door swished closed behind him and Sadie swiped the tears from her eyes.

Lyle knew it was his turn. He hoped he fared as well as the old man. "I'll be out of here in a few hours."

Sadie nodded. "You were lucky." Her lips trembled. "You protected me and you got shot."

"I had to protect you." He squeezed her hand. "I couldn't let him hurt you."

"I know. It's your job."

"Sadie." He waited until she met his gaze. "Yes, it's my job. Until this Barker situation is resolved, I'll be at your side every moment and I will make protecting you my top priority."

Disappointment flashed in her eyes.

"And when it's over, I'll still be here."

Tears slid down her cheeks, but the disappointment was gone. "You sure about that?"

"I have never been more sure of anything in my life." He pulled her down to him and gave her a kiss. "I love you, Sadie. I have since the first time I laid eyes on you."

She climbed in the bed on his good side and stretched out next to him. "Good," she said finally.

"Because I really didn't want to have to borrow one of Gus's shotguns."

Lyle kissed her forehead. "Does that mean you still love me, or do you just plan to keep me around to help you rebuild your house?"

"I haven't decided yet."

He frowned. Started to ask what that meant, but she turned his face to hers and smiled. "About rebuilding the house," she explained. She caressed his jaw and peered deeply into his eyes. "My life is a real mess right now, Lyle McCaleb, but the one thing that is crystal clear is how much I love you."

That was all he needed to hear. The rest they would figure out as they went.

So far it appeared they were in for a rough ride, but they were both prepared to hang on tight.

Chapter Sixteen

The Colby Agency, Houston, 6:00 p.m.

Victoria stared out the conference room window that overlooked Houston's unmistakable skyline. It wasn't Chicago, but it was beautiful nonetheless. She had spoken to Jim earlier today. Things were going well at the Chicago offices. Tasha and the children were anxious to see Victoria and Lucas as soon as they returned.

The transition here in Houston had gone very smoothly. Except for this case.

She turned and walked to the table that served as her desk. Clare Barker remained off their radar. Rafe had not come forward to give any additional information. Victoria couldn't determine whether he was shocked by his friend's betrayal or whether he had received the confirmation he needed and had nothing further to add.

They had found no other connection between Tony Weeden and the Barkers.

Victoria lowered into the chair and opened the file once more. She had pored over the information repeatedly and found nothing useful. And yet she had to be missing something.

Something that made the circle complete.

Rafe Barker had twenty-five days to live. How could they possibly hope to unravel this immensely complicated puzzle in that short time?

Perhaps she wasn't supposed to. The concept had crossed her mind that Rafe had attempted to use her agency to point his wife in the right direction. But that made no sense since Janet Tolliver was the one who knew the whereabouts of the daughters and Rafe had provided that contact.

What were they missing?

"It's time to call it a day, my dear."

The sound of Lucas's voice brought a smile to her lips. He was back! She stood and hugged him. "I'm so glad you're here."

He drew back and smiled for her. Victoria loved his smile. "Ah, but that's only because I lost our mark."

Victoria took his face in her hands and kissed him. "There was no way we could have known she had an accomplice who had set up that arrangement in advance of her release." Much had been revealed since the fire at the apartment complex.

Lucas ushered her into a chair before taking the one next to her. "The complex manager admitted that Weeden had made the arrangements months ago under the name Toni Westen. He leased one apartment with the guarantee that the other would be available for his friend. He gave the manager a hefty bonus."

Victoria doubted the manager would have confessed if not for the fire that had been traced back to Weeden's apartment. He had arrogantly left some of the materials he had used to stage the fire the way he wanted.

The police were searching for him and Clare Barker in connection to the fire.

"The entire sequence of events," Lucas shook his head, "was carefully planned and executed. Clare Barker knew she would be watched after her release."

Victoria didn't understand that part. "It's almost as if she knew exactly what Rafe would do when she was released."

Lucas gave a nod of agreement. "We may be the puppets and he may very well be the puppet master."

That was the part that worried her the most. "Oh, Lyle was released from the hospital. He's fine and insists he can continue providing protection for Sadie until this is resolved."

Lucas lifted a skeptical eyebrow. "From what Simon tells me, we may be losing him."

"I'm certain that's the case." The thought made Victoria smile, no matter that she hated to lose a fine investigator like Lyle.

"What we do for love."

Victoria mentally paused. "Do we have a love triangle here?"

"Are we talking about Lyle and Sadie or someone else?"

Victoria arranged the relevant photos on the conference table. "We have Rafe and Clare Barker. Tony Weeden and Janet Tolliver. Have Rafe and Clare planned this bizarre reunion all along? Or was it Clare and Tony? Tony and Janet? Or Janet and Rafe?"

"We found no evidence that Janet had ever worked for the prison system or had any contact whatsoever with Rafe or Clare since their arrests. Or before actually, other than the fact that Clare and Janet were separated as children."

"Weeden has never worked at Mountain View prison, where Clare was housed."

"Yet," Lucas countered, "there is a connection between Weeden and Clare. Obviously."

"Obviously," Victoria agreed as she surveyed the photos once more. "What does a thirty-three-year-old man have in common with a fifty-six-year-old woman?"

"Well, we can rule out money. The Barkers scraped by before their arrests. There is no hidden savings."

"The house was sold for unpaid taxes."

Lucas gathered up the photos and placed them in the file then closed it. "Our options are limited. We keep an eye out for Clare to surface again and we protect her daughters. That's basically all we can do other than keep digging."

"The other two are much more complicated situations." Victoria worried about Laney Seagers in particular. Life had not been easy on her. She trusted no one and there was a child involved.

"I'm confident the investigators chosen will be able to handle their assigned cases."

Victoria was, as well, for the most part. But the best investigator could not control the actions of an uncooperative principal.

"If Weeden had anything to do with the fire at Sadie's home and the warning message left for her," Lucas reminded her, "then Rafe Barker's assertions may prove true."

Billy Sizemore adamantly denied any involvement with those two malicious acts. But he was about as trustworthy as a snake lying in wait in the grass.

Victoria folded her arms over the case file so she wouldn't be tempted to look at it again.

"You're tired," Lucas suggested.

"I am." She gazed into her husband's wise gray eyes. "I keep asking myself what we're doing here."

He smiled. "We're finishing something we started."

"Perhaps I shouldn't have started this case, Lucas." She was tired. So very tired. They had made the decision to retire. To have a home in Texas as well as Chicago and travel back and forth at their leisure.

Yet, here they were deeply embroiled in perhaps one of the most complicated and heinous cases she had ever taken on.

How long would they be able to keep the media from intruding? The fire had already gotten Clare Barker a mention in the local news.

"My dear." He clasped her hands in his. "Your heart has always been your guide. Retirement will not change that. I don't want anything about you to change."

She lifted his hands and kissed each one. "We'll finish this together and then we'll take a nice long vacation."

"Promises, promises." He brushed a kiss against her lips.

A rap on the door interrupted their little moment. Simon visibly struggled with suppressing a smile. "I hope I'm not interrupting anything that won't wait."

Victoria stood. "Not at all. We were just discussing dinner."

Lucas stood, as well. "Perhaps you and Jolie would like to join us."

"Actually," Simon offered, looking and sounding a bit sheepish, "that's why I'm here. Jolie reminded me that I was supposed to invite you two to our house for dinner as soon as you were both here and available."

Victoria and Lucas exchanged a look. "We're free," Victoria said, "if you're certain this is not too short of a notice for Jolie."

Simon shook his head. "Trust me. She will be prepared. Since our move to Houston she has decided to stay home. She prepares at minimum a three-course meal each evening."

Lucas chuckled. "Sounds like you may need a raise, Ruhl."

Simon smiled. "That's the other thing. She has recently joined the extreme couponing movement. We now have stockpiles." He adjusted his tie. "It's quite unsettling."

They closed up the office and strolled across the parking lot. Victoria was glad to be out for the evening. She had spent far too much time cooped up with the case file of monsters.

She hooked an arm around the arm of each man. But there was no need to worry. The Colby Agency never failed a client. It wasn't going to start now.

At the car she glanced over her shoulder. She frowned. Strange. She had the oddest feeling that she was being watched.

This case was getting to her.
Tomorrow would be a better day.
It always was.

* * * * *

*Don't miss the next installment
of the Colby, TX trilogy,
HIGH NOON,
coming next month only from Harlequin Intrigue!*

SUSPENSE

COMING NEXT MONTH
AVAILABLE JUNE 12, 2012

#1353 WRANGLED
Whitehorse, Montana: Chisholm Cattle Company
B.J. Daniels

#1354 HIGH NOON
Colby, TX
Debra Webb

#1355 EYEWITNESS
Guardians of Coral Cove
Carol Ericson

#1356 DEATH OF A BEAUTY QUEEN
The Delancey Dynasty
Mallory Kane

#1357 THUNDER HORSE HERITAGE
Elle James

#1358 SPY HARD
Dana Marton

REQUEST YOUR FREE BOOKS!
2 FREE NOVELS PLUS 2 FREE GIFTS!

 Harlequin®

INTRIGUE®

BREATHTAKING ROMANTIC SUSPENSE

YES! Please send me 2 FREE Harlequin Intrigue® novels and my 2 FREE gifts (gifts are worth about $10). After receiving them, if I don't wish to receive any more books, I can return the shipping statement marked "cancel." If I don't cancel, I will receive 6 brand-new novels every month and be billed just $4.49 per book in the U.S. or $5.24 per book in Canada. That's a saving of at least 14% off the cover price! It's quite a bargain! Shipping and handling is just 50¢ per book in the U.S. and 75¢ per book in Canada.* I understand that accepting the 2 free books and gifts places me under no obligation to buy anything. I can always return a shipment and cancel at any time. Even if I never buy another book, the two free books and gifts are mine to keep forever.

182/382 HDN FEQ2

Name	(PLEASE PRINT)

Address	Apt. #

City	State/Prov.	Zip/Postal Code

Signature (if under 18, a parent or guardian must sign)

Mail to the **Reader Service:**
IN U.S.A.: P.O. Box 1867, Buffalo, NY 14240-1867
IN CANADA: P.O. Box 609, Fort Erie, Ontario L2A 5X3

Not valid for current subscribers to Harlequin Intrigue books.

**Are you a subscriber to Harlequin Intrigue books
and want to receive the larger-print edition?
Call 1-800-873-8635 or visit www.ReaderService.com.**

* Terms and prices subject to change without notice. Prices do not include applicable taxes. Sales tax applicable in N.Y. Canadian residents will be charged applicable taxes. Offer not valid in Quebec. This offer is limited to one order per household. All orders subject to credit approval. Credit or debit balances in a customer's account(s) may be offset by any other outstanding balance owed by or to the customer. Please allow 4 to 6 weeks for delivery. Offer available while quantities last.

Your Privacy—The Reader Service is committed to protecting your privacy. Our Privacy Policy is available online at www.ReaderService.com or upon request from the Reader Service.

We make a portion of our mailing list available to reputable third parties that offer products we believe may interest you. If you prefer that we not exchange your name with third parties, or if you wish to clarify or modify your communication preferences, please visit us at www.ReaderService.com/consumerschoice or write to us at Reader Service Preference Service, P.O. Box 9062, Buffalo, NY 14269. Include your complete name and address.

HI11B

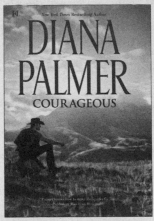

*Harlequin® Romantic Suspense presents the final book
in the gripping* PERFECT, WYOMING *miniseries
from best-loved veteran series author Carla Cassidy*

*Witness as mercenary Micah Grayson and cult escapee
Olivia Conner join forces to save a little boy and to take
down a monster, while desire explodes between them....*

Read on for an excerpt from
MERCENARY'S PERFECT MISSION

Available June 2012 from Harlequin® Romantic Suspense.

"**I** won't tell," she exclaimed fervently. "Please don't hurt me. I swear I won't tell anyone what I saw. Just let me have my other son and we'll go far away from here. I'll never speak your name again." Her voice cracked as she focused on his gun and he realized she believed he was Samuel.

Certainly it was dark enough that it would be easy for anyone to mistake him for his brother. When the brothers were together it was easy to see the subtle differences between them. Micah's face was slightly thinner, his features more chiseled than those of his brother.

At the moment Micah knew Samuel kept his hair cut neat and tidy, while Micah's long hair was tied back. He reached up and pulled the rawhide strip, allowing his hair to fall from its binding.

The woman gasped once again. "You aren't him...but you look like him. Who are you?" Her voice still held fear as she dropped the stick and protectively clutched the baby closer to her chest.

"Who are you?" he countered. He wasn't about to be taken in by a pale-haired angel with big green eyes in this evil place where angels probably couldn't exist.

HRSEXP0612

"I'm Olivia Conner, and this is my son Sam." Tears filled her eyes. "I have another son, but he's still in town. I couldn't get to him before I ran away. I've heard rumors that there was a safe house somewhere, but I've been in the woods for two days and I can't find it."

Micah was unmoved by her tears and by her story. He knew how devious his brother could be, and Micah would do everything possible to protect the location of the safe house. There was only one way to know for sure if she was one of Samuel's "devotees."

Will Olivia be able to get her son back from the clutches of evil? Or will Micah's maniacal twin put an end to them all? Find out in the shocking conclusion to the PERFECT, WYOMING *miniseries.*

MERCENARY'S PERFECT MISSION
Available June 2012, only from
Harlequin® Romantic Suspense, wherever books are sold.

Harlequin® Blaze™
red-hot reads

Fall under the spell of fan-favorite author

Leslie Kelly

Workaholic Mimi Burdette thinks she's satisfied dating the handsome man her father has picked out for her. But when sexy firefighter Xander McKinley moves into her apartment building, Mimi finds herself becoming…distracted. When Mimi opens a fortune cookie predicting who will be the man of her dreams, then starts having erotic dreams, she never imagines Xander is having the same dreams! Until they come together and bring those dreams to life.

Blazing
Midsummer Nights

The magic begins June 2012

Saddle up with Harlequin® series books this summer and find a cowboy for every mood!

Available wherever books are sold.